Daddy's Boy

Johannes T. Evans

Fantasy/Crime. The youngest son of the family business struggles for the approval of his father.

In the magical smuggling town of Lashton, the youngest son of the Laithes, a prominent crime family, struggles to make himself heard and accepted by his family, especially his father. At the age of 17, he undergoes a metamorphosis.

23k, rated E for violence, featuring Dai Laithe, Oidhche Laithe, and the rest of the Laithe family, with some appearances from Gellert Osgodby and to a lesser extent, Lucien Pike.

Please note that this is a violent piece about broadly abhorrent men throughout, and it contains a lot of content that may be triggering, particularly severe PTSD, anxiety, graphic violence, murder, and complex family dynamics including neglect and a survival of the fittest mentality.

Daddy's Boy is a work of fiction created from the author's imagination. Any resemblance to living persons, living or dead, or resemblance to actual events, places, or names is purely coincidental.

Daddy's Boy

Oidhche leaned back on the bed, spreading luxuriously on grey silk sheets. It was a very warm morning, and they were cool and satiny-smooth under the skin of his naked back, a pleasant relief; it was still dark outside, but the skies were beginning to lighten from a pitch and moonless black to a smoky purple.

Dunnock had climbed out of bed, and Oidhche pulled himself up to recline against the pillows, his hands loosely folded over his belly, as he watched him get up.

Dunnock moved with the smooth, easy confidence of a man who wasn't old enough yet to worry too much about how people might look at his body. Completely naked and shining with sweat, Oidhche could see the come dripping down his thighs, wet and filmy where it dripped out of his well-used cunt.

Dunnock's back rippled with muscle – he'd been a gymnast, when he was a little girl, and Oidhche remembered seeing the pictures of him competing in different competitions around Cymru-Loegr, and then internationally. Pride of Lashton, so he'd been, before he'd cracked under the pressure and the surveillance, spiralled on a cocktail of pixie dust and benzos, realised he wasn't a girl, chopped his budding tits off, and started killing people.

That was a bit of simplification, but Oidhche was a man who liked simple explanations, and a simple explanation was all he needed.

Dunnock's shoulders were broad compared to his waist, which was narrow and square and had an exaggerated V cutting in against his hips. Touching his body was a fascinating study in anatomy, feeling the hard weight of his pectorals, the carved-out shape of his abdominal muscles, the power in his thighs and his biceps, but Oidhche's favourite was in the impossible strength of his shoulders, how they were packed with muscle like a carthorse's.

Oidhche normally liked to have Dunnock fuck his arse – he liked muscular men, liked how hard they could fuck him, drive him down into the mattress until he was bruised from his very core, but last night he'd fucked into Dunnock from behind, taken him doggy style, all the better to admire the ripple and shift of the muscles in his back.

Now, whenever Dunnock fucked him, Oidhche would have the perfect mental image of the muscle working to let him piston into him, would be able to perfectly visualise Dunnock's terrific shoulders, all that power.

"You having a demented episode, old man?" asked Dunnock coldly, and Oidhche looked up from his musings, blinking placidly at Dunnock.

"You know, baby, it's not very nice to mean to Daddy," said Oidhche. "You might hurt his feelings."

"Oh no," said Dunnock flatly. "Whatever will I do if Daddy's feelings are hurt? I should perish from the shame." He said it so bluntly, and with such venomous sarcasm, that Oidhche chuckled, stretching out his arms and feeling the pleasant pull in his tired muscles before he sat up.

"You ask me a question?"

"You want me to take out Verdance Pike?" he asked. He was leaning forward as he wiped a wet cloth up the inside of his thighs and against his open lips before leaning back and doing the same to his arse. Funny, how something so basic could be appealing in such a primal way, could make Oidhche want to summon him back to bed and fuck him.

Shame that his old bones – or, more importantly, his old cock and balls – just didn't have the refractory period to allow for that kind of indulgence these days, not unless he took something for it alongside the pixie dust, and at his age, he had to take care not to go about *asking* for a heart attack, which was exactly what that would be.

"For dinner?" asked Oidhche, and Dunnock scoffed, rolling his eyes. Tossing the cloth into the bathroom, where it landed with a distant splat in the bath, Dunnock picked up his shirt and began to dress himself.

Dunnock never liked to stay the night, and when he did, it wasn't in Oidhche's bed – Oidhche'd never much cared for the needy boys, the ones who wanted to be held or the ones that wanted to hold him, and Dunnock was far too nasty a little cunt to want for that sort of thing. Now and then, these past few months, he'd take a little cat nap in Oidhche's office, lie straight back on the chaise and go uncomfortably still as he slept, but that was a relief compared to when they wanted to linger in Oidhche's bed or wrap themselves around him. It was why he was dressing himself now, when it was almost three in the morning, to go off and do whatever he did – Dunnock wouldn't go home to his little flat on the beach front until it was at least five, and he'd be out again, bright and bushy-tailed and ready to spatter someone's blood on a wall, by nine.

"Why would I want you to take him out, baby? What's Verdance Pike ever done to me?"

"He's a Pike. Isn't that enough?"

Oidhche tutted disapprovingly, watching Dunnock step into his jeans and pull them up the long length of his legs – Oidhche was a tall man himself, taller than Dunnock was, even, but his was a lanky and gangling height, and although he'd grown into it, although he loped like the wolf he'd come to be, his body would never ripple with the strength that Dunnock's did. Oidhche was a swimmer, even did pilates twice a week, but even at Dunnock's age, he could never have flourished like *he* did, and—

Mm, why would he want to? It was nice to appreciate what you didn't have, and Oidhche's nasty little songbird ate like a shrike, all that *meat,* to keep his muscles in place.

"You know, a thing that you're going to have to learn, sweetheart, is that you can't just go around killing everybody on the other side. That's bad business."

"We eliminate the other side," said Dunnock. "Less competition. How's that not good business?"

"Eliminate the other side," said Oidhche, and laughed, tapping his fingers against his thigh. "What gives a boy like you so much ambition?"

"I was a professional athlete," said Dunnock.

"Oh, yeah," said Oidhche thoughtfully. "Guess that'll do it."

Dunnock exhaled an almost-laugh out through his nose, nocking his belt shut, and rolled his shoulders.

"Speaking of being a professional athlete," said Oidhche, "I don't suppose it has anything to do with that trophy the boy is bringing home to his daddy, that he won in that fancy little ice-skating competition last month?"

Dunnock scowled. "I never did ice-skating," he said coldly. "My main pursuits were the beam and vault."

"Mm," agreed Oidhche. "The Pike boy's better than you at those as well, isn't he?"

Dunnock scoffed. "Can I ask you a question?" he asked.

"Sure, baby, what do you want to know?"

"The fuck kind of name is Oidhche?"

"Well, I don't know, what the fuck kind of name is Dunnock?"

"It's a bird."

"Uh huh."

Dunnock shrugged powerful shoulders. "I like birds," he said.

When Oidhche had first carried on a conversation with Dunnock, he hadn't really believed he could be so fucking simple. Dunnock had been making a name for himself the past few years – he'd come out of rehab at seventeen, hair cropped short, hormones burning a hole in his back pocket because he was used to getting his medicine privately and Mommy wasn't so interested in bankrolling for baby now that baby was a boy and he wasn't bringing home trophies any longer.

Oidhche really didn't know what the boy's first job had actually been, because half a dozen people, suits and thugs alike, claimed to be the ones who'd hired him for his first – depending on who you asked, he'd either started out in the boxing ring in Albert's, and "accidentally" punched a guy so hard he'd snapped a bone in his neck and sent him packing, or with Petty O'Keefe, who he'd stabbed in the ear with a snapped cocktail stirrer, or with some French smuggler out of a pontoon boat coming in during a storm, or, or, or.

It didn't matter who he'd started with: it mattered that Dunnock took money for a kill, took cash for the services of his big, scary muscles and his attractive arsenal of blades and arrows, and that when people tried to kill *him*, it didn't go well for them.

He'd heard of the boy getting taken into the fold – one of the kids had mentioned it, that they'd started sparring with Dunnock at the gym, and that they'd invited him to join the payroll, but it had been one of the youngest who'd mentioned it. Who? Dag, Siân? Gearóid, maybe?

It didn't matter much – what mattered was that Oidhche knew Dunnock by sight, and the muscle boy he'd been playing with, a big old cowboy called Utah who was just a little too soppy for his liking, had already been going out of favour, and so he'd bought the boy a drink. Dunnock, polite thing, had taken it, and he'd answered every single question Oidhche had asked him – about the fancy school he'd gone to, about competing in gymnastics, about doing drugs, about killing people.

He just gave his answers so frankly, so honestly, so plainly, that it was hard to believe he was being real, but Oidhche had come to learn that Dunnock really *was* just that shallow a man, and really did think that simply.

He wasn't stupid, but while his plain thinking wasn't always a boon – times like this, for example, when he thought killing every

non-Laithe in Lashton was the answer to competing business needs –
when he decided to be the tactless little shit he was, it was refreshing.

"You like birds," said Oidhche contentedly. "Well, my mother liked
stars. My brothers and sisters, they had names like Reálta, Méa, Cúpla,
Gabhar."

Dunnock frowned, wrinkling up his nose and tilting his head to the
side. "An gabhar is a goat, isn't it?"

Dunnock had next to no Gaelic, which Oidhche knew the kids
teased him about, and appeared to have learned his farm animals to
amuse them as much to amuse himself.

Oidhche laughed. "Capricorn, baby. Sign of the sea-goat."

"Hm," grunted Dunnock.

"Oidhche Dhuibhré," said Oidhche. "I was born on a dark and
moonless night, no stars at all. She thought it was fitting to name me
thus."

"It was, wasn't it?" asked Dunnock. "You killed all your brothers
and sisters."

Oidhche chuckled, putting his hand on his chin and looking at
Dunnock and his big complicated muscles and his big simple brain
with affection. "You know, baby, that's not a nice thing to say to
Daddy."

"Daddy can't handle the truth?" asked Dunnock. "You did it."

"I did it," agreed Oidhche. "I didn't kill all of them – Reálta's
alive, she works out of Edinburgh. Works in a planetarium. And if
everyone had made a smart choice like she did, and got out of my
fucking business, they'd still be alive too."

"If your kids started killing each other, you'd spank them silly," said
Dunnock.

"I'd do more than that," said Oidhche mildly, putting out his hands,
and Dunnock, well-trained by now, picked up the glass of lemon ice
water on the dresser and poured him a glass, watching him drink. "But
my kids don't have a reason to kill each other – things are different to

how they used to be. The only thing that can go wrong for them is if they don't pick out which one of 'em is gonna lead – and to be honest with you, sweetheart? Which one leads won't be my problem. I'll be dead by then."

"What happens if one of them kills you?" asked Dunnock.

"Well, that'd be a shoe-in for leadership, I suppose," said Oidhche, considering the thought. He didn't think any of the kids would try that, but it was an interesting thought, and with nine custom-built little murderers still standing, it was a question of odds as much as anything else.

Well.

Eight.

But even then, the odds were interesting ones.

"I don't think any of them would kill you," said Dunnock, pouring a glass of water for himself before he poured Oidhche some more, and when Dunnock sat down on the bed, he sat cross-legged at the foot of it, a few inches between Oidhche's foot and Dunnock's crossed legs, so that they weren't touching each other. "Huw would be the most likely to do it, I think, but he'd overthink it if he did it alone, sabotage himself – he'd have to work in a pincer formation. Him on one side, and someone who balances out his temper on the other side – Dag, maybe, if he got less anxious in a few more years, but I don't think he'd step against you, and Dag is too close to Siân, who'd only kill you if she felt you'd earned it. Huw and Bridie would be the most dangerous combination."

"Too bad they fucking hate each other," said Oidhche, and Dunnock laughed this time. It was a funny little laugh he had, a bouncy little giggle too low and hoarse to be something Dunnock did regularly, but there was something endearing in it.

"That on purpose?"

"Mmm, no, not really, dice just shook out that way," said Oidhche. "Huw doesn't like me because I moved on too quickly after his mother and I split up – Bridie doesn't like me because after *her* mother died, I started up again too quickly, and started on boys instead of ladies, didn't want any more kids. They don't like each other because Huw's an everyday misogynist, and Bridie fucking terrifies him. Don't know what made him that way – I don't think I ever taught him to be scared of women, or to hate them the way he does. If Bridie wants to kill me, I hope she does it on her own – or goes with Huw, and then kills him. She deserves it more than he does."

"You're a real feminist," said Dunnock, in a voice that could easily be misconstrued as earnest if one didn't know he was incapable, and Oidhche sipped at his drink, resting the glass on his naked thigh and feeling the ring of cool condensation it left on his skin.

"Would you take the job if one of them paid you?"

"To kill you?"

"Yeah," said Oidhche.

Dunnock considered the question very seriously, giving it a lot of internal attention, which Oidhche liked – if he'd answered right away, it would have been disingenuous, regardless of what the answer was. "I suppose there's always a price," said Dunnock. "But it would have to be a high one – you're very healthy for your age, eat well, stay active, and your mind is sharp, keen. What are you, seventy?"

"Sixty-six, honey," said Oidhche chidingly, with a slight frown, and Dunnock's sly smile showed that he'd aimed high in his estimate on purpose.

"You're going to make eighty, if not eighty-five, before you retire – or die off, or get sick. That's my guess. It seems to me it would be more lucrative to stay with the Laithes – you'll get bored of me fucking you, but you take care of your boys, don't you?" He paused, but he wasn't waiting for an answer to the question, was just thinking a little more about what he was saying, so Oidhche didn't cut in. "It's not as though I'm hoping to put a ring on your finger, or beg that you keep me on a pretty little diamond leash. By the time it's right for one of your children to take over, I'll be well-poised to help guide our operation into a new era, same as them, give my support as a lieutenant. If I killed you now at one of their behests, perhaps it would be a quicker promotion, but my position would be, uh. I don't know. More precarious. If one of them kills you themselves, that's between family, but if I do it, there's no excuse. I'd be highly disposable, I think, and I don't like looking over my shoulder."

"You're not even gonna pretend you wouldn't kill me because you've got some feeling for me in that jacked little chest of yours?" he asked, and Dunnock looked at him critically.

"You wanted me to talk about feelings?" asked Dunnock, so surprised he *did* sound genuine. "I thought it was a business question."

"Oh, it was," said Oidhche. "And I appreciate good business. Who's your money on for head of the family after I die off, hm? You like to flutter on the horses, don't you?"

"I do," said Dunnock. "I play long odds, though. That means if I'm betting money on anybody, I'm betting money on your boy Dafydd."

Oidhche started to laugh, tipping back onto the bed. Dunnock, smirking, leaned back against the footboard, and they talked for a little while longer.

* * *

Dai Laithe woke, as he did a few nights a week, with a scream tearing raggedly out of his throat. His body was so soaked with sweat that the pyjamas he'd worn to bed – he couldn't stand to sleep in something as light as a t-shirt, even on hot nights like the last one – were almost transparent.

It was still early enough that it was barely light outside, but the door opened into his bedroom anyway, and Dag half-stumbled as he shoved his head into the room and squinted at him in the dark.

"You okay?" he asked, voice hoarse with sleep – he was naked except for his boxers and the chain around his neck, and compared to Dai, there was barely any sweat on him.

"Yeah," said Dai, sitting up in bed. He felt like he was about to be sick, his stomach roiling with it, and he was trembling hard. Now that he was awake, he was aware of how cold he was, so wet he might as well have been swimming, and he pulled himself out of bed. He didn't miss the way his brother looked him up and down for a second, and he snapped, "It wasn't a night terror, and I didn't fucking piss myself."

"Okay," said Dag, nodding his head, and he closed the door again. Dai stripped off his pyjamas, grabbing clothes, and as usual he was the first in the shower, and the first down into the kitchen.

His hands were still shaking a little after he drank his coffee, but they weren't full-bodied tremors any more – he still used the mandoline to julienne peppers, and as he was frying off a packet of lardons, he kept wearing the steel glove to grate the cheese, and he was glad of it every time he lost his grip on the block and his thumbs and forefingers dragged and pulled against the steel-cut edges of the plate.

He expected it to be Dag when he heard the noise on the stairs, but instead he saw Dunnock, his dad's most recent boy toy.

It was fucked, that he'd started at that. He'd divorced Huw, Cassian, and Trevyn's mother to remarry theirs, and that had been one thing – it had been another entirely when Mam had died, and he'd started fucking bodybuilders.

Male bodybuilders.

Dai had only been ten or eleven the first time he'd heard Bridie arguing with him about it, and he distantly remembered there being boys in the house that were Bridie's age, and never knowing whether they were her boyfriends or his.

Dunnock was built just like the rest of them were, tall and broad-shouldered and with a narrow waist, stacked with so much muscle he rippled with it. His jaw was just as cut as the others had been, but he was younger than usual, and he couldn't grow a beard yet, which his dad usually liked.

Dunnock Wesson was nineteen years old, only two years older than Dai, and he stank of sex and Dai's dad's cologne.

He was shimmying into the leather jacket he always wore – it was leather from a butter cow, bright yellow, and it made the yellow of his hair seem all the more gold, especially under the warm glow of the kitchen lights – as he came down to the bottom of the stairs, and Dai tried not to look at him too closely, at the tightness of his t-shirt and his jeans.

Dai puffed out his chest a little, raised his chin, and tried to sound casual as he asked, "Going to grace us with your presence for breakfast?"

It didn't sound the way it did when his dad said stuff like that – it didn't sound cool or disaffected or powerful. His voice sounded reedy and it shook even though he didn't stammer, and it sounded needy, too, like he *wanted* Dunnock to stay with them for breakfast.

"You're kind to invite me," said Dunnock, which Dai hadn't, but he bit down the urge to tell Dunnock that, because that was too defensive and he'd tried that before and Dunnock always gave him a haughty, superior look that made him feel like dying, "but for all your culinary skills, Dafydd, your portion sizes are made for the family of skinny rakes you come from. We can't all subsist on egg whites and vegetables."

"It's Dai," said Dai. "No one fucking calls me Dafydd."

"My mistake," said Dunnock with a smirk on his sculpted lips, putting his hands in his pockets, and sidled out of the door.

Dad came down the stairs a few minutes later, and he leaned on the kitchen counter, pointed to peppers, spinach, and some of the feta cheese that Dai had already cut into cubes, and Dai poured egg mixture into the frying pan.

He didn't have to cook breakfast.

His dad had told him that, once or twice, that he didn't have to cook breakfast, but that was always a trap, because if he *didn't* cook breakfast, the old man would say things like, "We really put you through that cute little hospitality school for nothing, huh?" and "Sweetheart, if you're not going to do some real work like the rest of us, the least you can do is make yourself useful around the house."

So Dai cooked breakfast.

"Heard you scream, honey," said Dad, leaning his chin against his hand and watching as Dai scattered ingredients into his omelette. "Nightmares *again*?"

"Sorry," said Dai, and Dad sucked his teeth, letting out a disapproving noise that made Dai's skin run suddenly cold, and he chanced a risk back at his face. Dad's lips had twisted into a small frown, and he was absently playing with the arms of his sunglasses, pushing them open and then closed again so that their gold shine caught the light.

"Oh, honey," he said disapprovingly, and Dai looked back to the omelette, turning up its edges. He could hear one of the showers running, probably Dag's, and he could hear the sound of the house starting to come to life, floorboards creaking upstairs as his brothers and sisters got out of bed. "Are you having these nightmares on purpose?"

"No," said Dai defensively.

"Then what the fuck are you apologising for?" Dad's voice remained sugar-sweet and perfectly even, but that just made it worse.

Dai closed his mouth with a quiet click, keeping his back to his father as he flipped over his omelette. He didn't know what to say to that, didn't know how to defend himself against it, so he listened to the sizzle of the eggs in the pan and the hum of the hob.

"See, baby," said Dad, "everyone can see you're..." He cleared his throat. "Well, you lack a little spine, hm? Shake like a little leaf, you stammer, you sweat. You already tell everyone you're weak before you open your mouth – you don't need to tell people by apologising for everything you can think of as icing on the cake."

"Yes, sir," said Dai dully, and he regretted it as soon as he said it, because it came out too quiet in almost a whisper and he knew that he hated, knew what was coming.

Dad sighed. "Talk to me like a man if you want to talk to me, baby," he said. "Acting scared of your own Daddy - what do you think I'm gonna do, hit you?"

Dai turned around, flipping the omelette onto a plate and cutting it in half so that his father could see the fluffy whiteness of the egg inside before he passed him his knife and fork.

"Think you've proved by now you don't need to hit somebody to hurt them," he said bluntly, and when his father looked at him in surprise, his eyebrows raised, Dai blanched. "Um, I mean, that is, I didn't mean, that's..."

His father's surprise turned back to a sort of tired disapproval, and he slightly curled his lip. "You know, for a second there, baby, I almost believed you were my son."

Dai turned around and took the tomatoes he'd been roasting out of the oven, just in time for when Dag came into the room and asked if Dai had made any.

* * *

It was a Wednesday morning, and they were busiest on Wednesday mornings.

They were all packed into the conference room, a lovely, glass-walled room in the centre of the company building, and as Oidhche sat back in his chair, one of his ankles loosely resting on his knee, spinning gently a few inches to the left and then to the right, the rest of the kids filtered into the room.

At Oidhche's left hand side, Dunnock amused himself by filing some of the blades he tended to secrete on his person to fine points.

Oidhche's personal favourite were the little needle-sized blades that folded out of his wristwatch, which Oidhche hadn't really believed could be lethal until he'd watched Dunnock drive two of them through someone's eye and directly, judging by the juice that came out, into their brain.

To Oidhche's right was Bridie – she and Huw typically rushed to beat one another to the punch, but Huw had been stuck in traffic, and had sloped into the room with a scowl when he'd realised she'd gotten there first – and the other kids were dotted around the table. Siân and Dag, the twins, were sitting together, as ever, leaning their heads together to play a game on Siân's phone, and Gearóid was beside them. Oidhche was fairly certain the boy was asleep, but he couldn't prove it – his eyes were open, but they'd glazed over in a way that looked wholly unnatural, and Oidhche was fairly certain they hadn't blinked in some time.

Trevyn was making no attempts to hide the fact that he was asleep, and Oidhche was certain that this was because he actually wasn't – Trevyn's head was nodded back in his chair, and his feet were resting in Cassian's lap. His eyes *were* closed, and now and then he would snore convincingly, but Oidhche knew that when the meeting commenced, he would open his eyes, sit up, and be perfectly attentive.

Cassian hadn't complained about Trevyn's feet being in his lap, and was resting his book on his brother's ankles; Huw, beside them, was rocking back and forth in his chair, one ankle rested on his knee, in much the same way Oidhche was, and was frowning down at his phone.

Ariana had her laptop in front of her, ready to make minutes, and Oidhche's personal assistant, Cerys, was sat beside her. The two of them were speaking quietly to one another, both of them looking at whatever was on Ariana's screen.

There were other people in the room, of course, but Dunnock and Cerys aside, it was only family that were really allotted a space at the table: crowded up against the walls and around the table were various officers, suppliers, some managers from some of their local businesses—

When Dai came into the room, a minute before nine, he had to wriggle between everyone else gathered, and Oidhche reserved the urge to actually release a sigh of embarrassment as he shakily burst out from between two of their accountants, and dropped heavily into the last seat left between Dunnock and Siân.

"Long queue?" asked Dunnock, and Dai gave him a very dirty look before sitting down in his seat and crumpling like a wet bag, his legs crossed over one another, his arms crossed over his chest, his shoulders hunched. When Oidhche looked at him, he could see that Dai was shivering slightly at all the attention, and he sighed heavily before he looked to Ariana at the opposite end of the table, and gestured for her to start.

Ariana liked chairing meetings, and what's more, she was good at it. Oidhche fondly remembered the first time she'd stomped confidently up to him in her little Mary Janes and stated, very clearly, that she thought that it was time for her to chair the meeting now, as he was getting so old he was virtually on the verge of death – and if he didn't see fit to *let* her chair the meetings, she would soon ensure he was.

She'd been nine.

Things had been going well, of late – of the five families in Lashton, the Laithes and the Kings were typically on top, in terms of legitimacy. They'd been doing well of recent in expanding into building up real estate between Lashton proper and the Llallwg Forest, and they'd been fucking the tax about on them, particularly when it came to the rental properties for students in Camelot.

They were smuggling, of course – what was a criminal enterprise in Lashton without a bit of smuggling? - and primarily trading in foodstuffs and alcohol that were in various ways restricted, but that was what the kids would call a *side hustle*.

Of the largest enterprises in Lashton, the Laithes were the only ones who didn't trade regularly in drugs and chemical highs, but that didn't mean they weren't affected by the markets.

Lucien Pike had recently found some new way to manufacture pixie dust very near to or in the city, and in recent months there'd been a sudden flood of the stuff onto the street – it was very high quality, and came in several ordinarily rare varieties. Oidhche had sampled it several times and been high off his tits each time in the most wonderful of ways, which was lovely.

What wasn't lovely was how stressed and irritable these market shifts had been making various of the Kings, and the Renns and the Sorrels were being pushed closer together by the resulting chaos – and Oidhche had already been distantly concerned they would soon intermarry, and this would only bring the two families closer together, which none of them needed.

"And that package of research samples came down from Edinburgh, but our alchemists can't take it," said Ariana.

"Why?" asked Oidhche.

"Among other reasons," said Bridie, "they're very unstable materials, and the alchemists are still rebuilding their roof. Rain water would add an unpredictable element. A lot of surveillance from the authorities, too," Bridie pronounced the word with a certain prejudice, "to ensure the rebuild is up to code. And they're unstable as fuck – we don't want them in the house."

"The Kings," said Dai, and then looked stunted, not finishing the sentence as they all turned to look at him. Under the pressure, he crumpled even more in his seat, looking closer to four feet than six, before he swallowed and sat up straight. Gritting his teeth, he said, "The Kings. Dandy King. He's got a, in the wholesaler's, a fucking, um. The walls, they're... Magically sealed, alchemically neutral, under a clean ward, so it's unreactive."

"How do you know?" asked Dunnock mildly, when no one else said anything, and Dai fidgeted in his seat.

"Courageous and Dandy King were talking about it at the pageant this Christmas. I overheard them talking – it's so that when they smuggle potions in other boxes or cans, disguised as other things, they don't have to worry so long as ingredients are kept separate."

"Okay," said Oidhche. "Well, Dandy owes you a favour, doesn't he, Huw?"

Huw nodded his head, drumming his fingers against the table. "After that thing in April, yeah. I can—"

"You don't have to go," interrupted Dai. "I can."

Huw, at being interrupted, leaned very slowly forward, and gave his little brother a uniquely venomous look. They were at opposite ends of the long table, diagonal to one another, and it was hardly where the opposites ended between them: where Dai had Oidhche's height and his dark colouring, his skin pale but olive-toned and his hair and eyes dark, Huw was as silver-blond as his mother was, and his flint eyes looked very hard as he pinned Dai with his gaze.

Between their ages, there was a separation of twenty-two years, and Oidhche thought it would be fair to say that of his siblings, Huw probably did hate Dai most – but then, who didn't hate him?

Siân and Dag loved him to pieces, of course, but they had to – they were creatures of habit – and Cassian liked him, and Bridie was capable of showing affection for him, whenever he was being quiet and sitting still.

Huw thought he was a snivelling little cunt, and in fairness to the man, he wasn't at all wrong.

"Beg pardon, Dafydd?" asked Huw coolly.

"You don't have to go to the t— trouble, I mean," said Dai, and he kept his chin raised high, not breaking eye contact with Huw, although he looked as though his eyes were about to start watering. Oidhche was almost impressed. "It's a minor errand. I can take it."

Huw rolled his eyes, and said, "I don't care. If you want to do it, do it."

Dai gave a stout little nod of his head, and before she noted this agreement down, Ariana looked down the centre of the table to Oidhche for his approval.

Oidhche shrugged, gave a vague wave of his hand, and Ariana wrote it down.

Later on, in his office, he sat back in his seat and ate his salad, thinking to himself. Dunnock had gone off to intimidate some witnesses, and all the kids had scattered off to do their own thing, as they liked to.

He had more meetings this afternoon, several of them online, which he didn't care for, but one of the benefits for the new pixie dust production on Pike's part was that a few more of their French and Breton contacts were recognising Lashton as more than just a port, and Oidhche was keen to capitalise on that.

When he'd first started out, in the middle of his siblings, where they'd all gone into more high-powered work – lawyers and bankers, for the most part, Méa a local councillor – he'd gone into selling real estate. He remembered fondly, sitting in the middle of the table, shrugging his shoulders and smiling placidly, feigning stupid when his brothers and sisters all laughed at him...

His mother had known. She'd known from the beginning that he wasn't as stupid as he pretended to be, that he understood more than he liked to let on, and he thought sometimes about the evenings he and her would spend together, him sitting back on the couch in this very office, her at her desk or looking out over Lashton from the balcony. They would talk, sometimes, about his classes or later, about the houses he was selling.

Oidhche sighed as he remembered the thrill he used to feel in those days, dropping just the right properties, or just the right tidbits, into conversation so that his siblings would pick them up and think that *they'd* come up with the idea to use them – dropping the right pieces of paperwork, helpfully chiming in with just the most useful piece of property law as if he didn't see the relevance, taking his sister to lunch by *just* the right place to snap up as a drop for certain goods.

He used to have such a good time of things, back then – there'd been nothing quite like playing his brothers and sisters against one another like they were little chess pieces, and none of them ever even *suspecting* that their brother had been playing them until later.

Reálta had known, but not until almost the end – that had been after Mama had died, God rest her soul, and he'd been close to losing his temper, hadn't schooled his feelings, hidden his real face, like he usually did, so that she saw him cold, saw him angry, and then saw him... satisfied.

She'd backed off right away, when she'd seen that, and they'd never spoken a word about it, not until everyone else was dead.

Oidhche didn't like to think of his kids doing what he'd done, but he didn't think it would ever come to that. He'd always taught them to play against one another, always encouraged them to look for each other's strengths and weaknesses, and as much as some of them quarrelled – or in Huw and Bridie's case, genuinely hated one another – they were too smart to get hung up on killing one another when they all knew how they could use each other, complement one another, balance each other out.

Except Dai, of course.

Oidhche looked at the big family photo on the wall.

They were all lined up, Oidhche with his arm around Saoirse, Dai in her arms – he was only five in this picture – and the rest of the kids all gathered around. He felt his lips curve up in a small smile at the look on Saoirse's face, in the photo: she was beaming, eyes sparkling, and her cheek was touching little Dai's, him clutching a chef's hat in his hand.

It was relaxed, that photo – Huw and Cassian had their arms around Trevyn's shoulders, with most of the youngest kids leaning up against their big half-brother's legs, and Huw had picked up Dag, where Cassian had not so much picked Morrigan up as she'd climbed to hang off him.

It was the last family photo they'd taken, all of them together – the next time so many of them had been lined up like that, it had been for the kids' funeral.

He remembered how sick it had made him, that day, going out of the church and into the yard, and seeing the four fresh dug graves on the family plot, all of them small ones – and he remembered how all he'd wanted was to go back to the hospital, because Dai was alone in the hospital room.

Imagine that, not wanting to go to your own kids' funerals.

Oidhche finished up his salad, put it aside, and pressed on the intercom.

"Cerys, could you send me in this week's Camelot portfolio?"

"Can do, Mr Laithe. There's an article in the Castle Herald about the academics' unions and rental prices, you want me to send that through too?"

"Oh, sweetheart, you know me to a T. Put another star in the bonus jar," said Oidhche, and when Cerys laughed, logging off the intercom, he smiled, spinning around in his chair.

He was getting old, he knew that. Swimming and salad and good sex would only get an old man so far – things were changing in Lashton, changing in the Laithes, and he wondered if he'd *like* to retire. He always felt like he'd taught the kids well enough that the right one would emerge as leader, but it just hadn't happened yet, and he wondered if he'd fucked up there, if he needed to do something else with them.

Retirement...

It sounded nice, but what would he be, with no work to do? The work was all he'd known for sixty years.

The last time he hadn't worked was when Dai was in hospital, and that...

Nah.

* * *

"D'you want us to go with you?" asked Siân.

"No," said Dai.

"I can give you a lift over," said Dag.

"No," said Dai. "Everyone thinks I'm a fucking pussy and I can't do anything, but if you don't *let* me do anything, how the Hell am I supposed to prove otherwise?"

"No one thinks you're a pussy, mate," said Dag. Siân and Dai both turned to look at him, and Dag looked powerlessly between them for a second before he crumpled slightly and said, "Alright, but no one'll think you're a *more* of a pussy if one of us goes with you."

"What, if I have one of you to come be my muscle?" asked Dai. His hands were shaking, and he felt like being sick as he tested the weight of the wood crate. It wasn't heavy, not at all – no matter how he looked, he did lift, and he was strong, when his grip could be trusted.

He had to go to the gym, normally exercised two or three hours every night, because if he was physically exhausted in combination with his anxiety medication, he didn't normally have the night terrors, and if he did, they were mild enough that he didn't piss himself or go out of a window.

He wanted, really, to have Dag or, better, Siân, to go with him. He didn't know who worked at Dandy King's wholesalers, but Dandy King himself was controlled and cool and genuinely really fucking terrifying even without the jacked tyre-rollers he kept as bodyguards, and Fanciful King was a pretty boy but he carried a fucking *sword* and he could use it, and he knew that the Kings hired—

Well.

He was scared of being stabbed or poisoned; he was scared of being bruised up or having his bones broken, because he'd had enough of that when he was a kid, and it wasn't even the getting hurt that fucked him up, but the *anticipation* of getting hurt, because he couldn't deal with it, couldn't prepare, and that was assuming he didn't just get killed.

It was a minor task.

It was fucking stupid to be as terrified as he was, because this was nothing, and the only reason they were letting him do it was *because* it was so minor, because whenever he tried to do something properly he fucked it up.

He remembered the last time he'd gone on the boat and sailed to one of the fae islands in the English Channel, and they'd gotten caught in a storm and he'd had a panic attack even before he hit the water, and then he'd nearly drowned, and that was years ago.

He'd never killed someone.

He'd never even hurt someone, not really – he could go for ages in the gym with his gloves on and a guard in his mouth, and he could put Dag or Siân down easy. Cassian would come head-to-head with him sometimes, and he was lethal on the streets, but Dai always won when they were in the ring together.

He'd never stabbed anybody, never cut anyone up, never even thrown a punch outside of the ring, but in theory, he could be good.

It was stupid, for him to be so terrified of fighting – in the ring, with family, no one would really hurt him, but outside, with random people, anything could happen to him, anything *would* happen to him, and it would *hurt*.

"You're breathing pretty heavy," said Siân.

"No, I'm fucking not!" snapped Dai, and picked up the crate.

He psyched himself up the whole walk over, just rehearsed exactly what he was going to say, exactly how he was going to say it – he wasn't going to stammer, he wasn't going to stutter, he wasn't going to fucking shake or sweat or hyperventilate or *freak out*.

He kept his breathing even, *forced* his breathing to stay even, so that his heartbeat stayed at a rhythm too, and by the time he shouldered his way into the wholesaler's, he felt good. Not confident, not exactly, but good, energised, ready.

It wasn't even Fanciful King behind the cashier's desk – it was some sweaty little lad, who was a foot shorter than Dai instead of just two inches, and Dai suppressed his smile as he strode forward, trying to mimic his father's wolfish lope, and set the crate down on the counter.

"How can I... how can I help you, um, sir?" asked the boy.

"Do you know who I am?" asked Dai coolly.

The boy swallowed hard. "Um," he said, "you're, um, you're a Laithe, sir."

"I'm *Dai* Laithe," said Dai. "Calling in a favour – Dandy owes us. *You* are going to take *this*. Just for a few days."

He pushed the crate slightly forward, and the cashier looked at it uncertainly. He was sweating profusely, trembling, and Dai almost felt like crowing in triumph, that it was *this guy*, and not him.

"Uh, I'm not really sure if I—"

"Did I sound like I was fucking asking permission?" demanded Dai – that wasn't as good, too sharp, too angry too soon, but the cashier didn't seem to take it as a lack of control, because he cringed away from Dai, and Dai's blood ran hotter in his veins with the satisfaction, the knowledge that this guy was seriously afraid of *him*.

He didn't turn when he heard the prim little steps on the metal staircase behind him, but the knowledge that someone else was approaching made a part of him panic, the idea of being pinned in by two people at once, and when he did turn, he turned his body as well as his head to look at the man who approached, so that he could back out more easily.

This wasn't Dandy King either – it was the wholesaler's manager, a nasty little bitch called Osgodby with glasses so thick he looked like a cartoon character. He'd been fucking Courageous King for a while, Dai knew that, because when he'd heard Courageous and Dandy talking that while ago, he'd come up.

He had a tight cunt, according to Courageous King, and dangerous teeth.

When he spoke, it was very cold and very sharp, like something held to a whetstone, and Dai had to restrain the urge to swallow, because this guy, unlike his cashier, was genuinely fucking dangerous: "How can we help you, Mr Laithe?"

All of the script that Dai had rehearsed fizzled out of his head at once, and his tongue felt heavy and thick in his mouth, his heart starting to speed under his suit. He was already slouching compared to a second ago, wasn't tall like he'd let himself be, and he almost grunted when he said, "Parcel."

Osgodby's eyes didn't blink behind his thick glasses, just stared at Dai very funny and weird and making Dai want to dig his way under the earth and fucking die there. He was starting to sweat himself, now, clammy wetness building up on the back of his neck, under the suit that never seemed to fit him, because he got nervous when the tailors started touching his chest or his back, and couldn't stand being measured.

"Yes, I see that," said Osgodby in a sort of easy, placid voice that Dai desperately wished he could replicate, didn't turn to look at the box. "What has it to do with us?"

"You're looking after it," Dai blurted out. It was clumsy, and he tried to remember what he'd literally *just* said to the cashier, whatever he'd said because he'd sounded good, sounded clever and confident and a little scary and now he wasn't any of that, now he was shaking, now he couldn't remember how to string three words together and he wanted to cry or scream or run and he couldn't do any of that without looking like a pussy. He didn't know what possessed him to lean forward, over Osgodby – Dai was six foot tall exactly, though he knew no one ever remembered him that tall, that they remembered him way shorter –

and growl, "And if you know what's good for you, you'll put it right aside. Speccy little cunt."

For a beat, there was silence, and Dai thought with relief that he'd managed to regain his momentum, that he'd managed to come off as cool and nasty and powerful again, but the cashier gasped in what sounded like horror, and that made him falter.

Why horror?

What had he seen Osgodby do before that Dai hadn't?

To Dai's relief, Osgodby seemed to relent, and he said in a smooth and unoffended voice, "Of course. Come with me, Mr Laithe, and I'll show you precisely where we'll set it aside for you."

Osgodby picked up the crate, and Dai repressed the want to actually let out a physical sigh of relief as he walked just behind Osgodby. He just wanted to go home, wanted to get this done and go home and not do anything for a while, but at least he'd done something, at *least*—

"It needs to be dry," said Dai as they came right back up to the door, where a little mat and a bin for umbrellas were waiting – when it was windy, some of the rain came in, and that wouldn't do at all.

"Does it?" asked Osgodby. He sounded almost cheerful, a friendly smile on his face that didn't look right there, that looked fucking *uncanny* there, and then he balanced the crate on his hip and pulled open the door, making the bell jingle.

It had made him flinch when he'd come in the wholesaler's earlier, and it made him shiver now, nausea surging up his throat and almost making him gag. "What the *fuck* are you—"

Osgodby threw the crate hard enough that it sailed over the stairs Dai had walked up to come into the shop, and when it hit the cobbled stones of the street outside, the wood splintered, bottles breaking and reacting with each other. Immediately, he could see a rainbow of technicoloured poisons spreading out into the gaps in the weather-polished brick, and he was so angry he almost felt like he'd black out with it.

He stepped to Osgodby, his hands moving of his own accord with the fury bubbling in his veins, and growled, "You can't *fucking*—"

Osgodby, for all he was short, was strong.

He used Dai's height against him, tripping him and then pushing the weight of his top half forward, and Dai shouted and tried to grab at something for purchase, but his legs had been thrown out from under him, and Osgodby had shoved him hard enough that, like the crate did, he sailed over almost every step, and landed hard on top of the mess.

He let out a scream of pain and rage as the wood and glass splintered further under his feet, shards of glass cutting up his neck and his arms and stabbing through the fabric of his shirt, and that was before the poisons – most of them were contact poisons that they'd been experimenting with, mild ones to discourage loitering in certain areas, a custom paint to mix onto benches in their new housing estates and parks so that only the people who lived around could sit; a few others were far stronger ones, meant for interrogation.

Of course, no one was meant to experience them all at once, let alone with open wounds, and Dai had to really grind his teeth to keep from screaming as the burn started, and then intensified.

He couldn't even focus on the camera flash of Miri Sorrel and Gus Renn's phones as he shakily tried to pull himself to his feet, and with hands trembling so hard he couldn't even grip it, he tried to dial a number into his phone.

* * *

Oidhche had come directly from the office, and when one of the guards at the house came to greet him, he shoved straight past him, taking the steps down into the basement.

When he'd built the house, he'd thought the pool would be nice, convenient, a little safer for when he or the kids wanted to swim in the mornings. He swam himself most mornings, and the kids all swam regularly, for the most part.

Not Dai.

Dai used the gym, but he couldn't stand water, started shaking so hard with anxiety that he couldn't keep himself above the surface, started gasping even before he was drowning – he wasn't downstairs for the pool.

Dunnock was on his feet, his shoulders leaning back against the wall beside the archway, and Oidhche stepped through the gap, his lips pressed together, and although he made no external show of his surprise, he felt himself inwardly shock at the sight of his youngest son.

Dai was sitting forward on one of the benches, two sprays of water rushing down over his skin. His chest and his back were already a mess of scars, cut open where they'd had to put his fucking ribs back after the crash, and all the years that had passed hadn't made the scars less obvious, just smoothed out their texture somewhat – they cut him through from various angles like he was a diagram at the butcher's, and now, they were decorated with a great many smaller, jagged wounds.

Most of them wouldn't stop bleeding, and Oidhche wasn't sure if that was because whatever potion mixes he'd had burned into him had anti-coagulant properties, or if it was because Cassian had cast something on him to keep him bleeding, to make sure whatever poison was in the cuts was washing out again.

Dai was naked, blood running down his chest, and in between the new cuts and the old scars, Oidhche could see the places where the skin was alive with painful red rashes, parts of his skin dyed green and purple and blue with magical burns; fully-clothed beside him, just outside of the spray but visibly damp from the water, Dag was holding his hand, and Cassian was tending to him as though he didn't even notice the water rushing over him, soaking his clothes. Cassian's hands were glowing with power as he worked, and Dai was so shut down he wasn't even shivering, wasn't even *blinking*.

He was just staring forward like he was in some kind of fugue, didn't notice his father watching even though Dag and Cassian did, and Oidhche stepped out of the hot steam of the shower room, his hands clenching at his sides.

"Siân has salvaged about half of the box," said Dunnock quietly. "The bottles that survived – she's taken them to an alchemist outside of town to take care of, and she's sent word to our team, advising that the bottles were damaged and that we need new samples. They'll have more to ha—"

"Who the fuck did this?" interrupted Oidhche, and Dunnock, very calm, met his gaze.

Dunnock had taken off his jacket, which rested in the shower room in the pile with Dai's clothes, but Oidhche could see that his shirt front was stained with Dai's blood and a mix of magical dyes.

Dai had called Siân, of course, but Dunnock had been going that way, and it had been him that had picked Dai up and carried him home, calling on Cassian that there was a family medical emergency. From the quick, aborted summary that Dag had given Oidhche on the phone, by the time Dunnock had picked Dai up, he'd been completely out of it, eyes open, but not really conscious.

"Gellert Osgodby," said Dunnock. "He's the manager of the King wholesaler's."

"The Kings share him between them," said Oidhche, feeling himself frown. "Courageous King was fucking him a while, although that's died off now – he's a nasty little cunt. It was him that killed Gwyn Fickle."

Dunnock looked at him sceptically. "You sure? He doesn't look like he could kill a pigeon."

"Looks can be deceiving," said Oidhche, nodding to the shower room. "Nine children left, thirteen overall, and *he's* the one that looks most like me."

Dunnock closed his mouth, and he looked Oidhche up and down in a way that Oidhche didn't like. It wasn't predatory, nor particularly analytical: there was a distance in Dunnock's eyes he didn't often see, a slight twist on his perfect little mouth.

"You want me to kill him?" he asked softly.

"Osgodby?"

"Mm."

"No," said Oidhche. "If we kill him right off the bat, we show this has hurt us. We'll have him tarred and feathered – I'll have Huw talk to Dandy. Like we should have done in the fucking first place. Of all the things I didn't realise the boy could fuck up!"

Oidhche stalked back toward the stairs, and Dunnock followed after him up the stairs and into the other room.

"He's going to be alright," said Dunnock as they came into the lounge, and Oidhche turned to glare at him. Dunnock, unaffected, went on, "A few burns, the cuts. It's the humiliation he most has to worry about – the kids thaw saw him were made up largely from the Renn and Sorrel families, all of them his age, sixteen, seventeen, eighteen."

"I don't need you coddling my fucking feelings."

"He's your son," said Dunnock. "It's natural to be worried about him."

Oidhche lunged, and Dunnock didn't flinch as Oidhche's hand wrapped tight around his throat, shoving him back against the wall. Dunnock went easy, didn't resist as Oidhche crowded him back.

"You're a good fuck, sweetheart," said Oidhche softly, "but you're not so good you get to comment on what goes on around here. You're not *part* of this family – you're an accessory, for me, my favourite toy. That can change *real* quick."

"He's going to be okay," said Dunnock again, in the same tone, and Oidhche squeezed tight around his throat. "I can kill the manager for you if you want him dead, Daddy. No one has to know. I can make it look like an accident – make it seem like it has nothing to do with this." Dunnock's fingers were slowly tracing up the surface of Oidhche's chest, playing over the buttons, and Oidhche was almost tempted – almost, but not quite.

"We'll tar and feather him," said Oidhche, and before Dunnock could go on, Oidhche kissed him, kissed him fiercely, and let Dunnock start guiding him back to one of the bedrooms.

* * *

It took a few days for Dai to start talking again.

The Osgodby lad hadn't been tarred or feathered, as it turned out – he'd disappeared right off the fucking map, initially, and soon after, he'd re-emerged as the new secretary to Lucien Pike.

Oidhche didn't like that.

He didn't like what it boded at all, because it meant Pike had picked Osgodby out special, that something about him appealed, and Pike usually picked his secretaries based on how appealing they looked to stick his cock into. While Oidhche had no doubt he'd be stuffing his new secretary with cock at some point – Pike was not so much bisexual as he was an opportunist – it was plain that he hadn't been selected with cock in mind, and that... That wasn't good.

It was best for all of them when Lucien Pike thought with his cock: when his brain came into play, he became a good deal more dangerous for everybody.

Siân and Dag had gone to intimidate Osgodby the first time he'd come home, and when Dag had gone to grab him, Osgodby had bent back some of his fingers – and when that hadn't made them back down, Pike had picked Dag up on a routine dock inspection, and returned him bloody.

Dag was fine, *would* be fine, had seemed more embarrassed at having cracked under the pain than really rattled by it, and Oidhche saw no reason to further the back and forth, encourage the Pikes to strike back at them.

Osgodby was theirs now, and the Pikes guarded their own like feral dogs guarded rotten pieces of bone – their blood was rabid, each of them as unstable as the next, even before they started fucking each other, and Oidhche didn't fancy starting a war over a secretary that, by all accounts, had only thrown Dai out because Dai had insulted him first, like the stupid little prick that he was.

When Oidhche went into Dai's room, he didn't knock, just pushed the door open.

He was dressed in his funny little dark blue pyjamas, so that for a second, Oidhche looked at him and saw the tired little boy with bandages around his head and a brace on his neck, wheezing in his hospital bed. He'd barely been able to stand being in that room, had left most of it to Saoirse, because as much as he'd wanted to reach out and cradle him, to touch him, he couldn't until the braces all came off, in case they hurt him – and by the time they *could*, by the time he *could* touch Dai again, hold him, it was...

It wasn't so simple any more.

For most of the kids, having Daddy hold them, give them a hug, even now, that meant safety, love – even Huw relaxed when Oidhche hugged him or carded a hand through his hair, no matter that he might spit at him after. It didn't matter what you did to Dai: he shook like a beaten dog regardless, and it made Oidhche angry to his core, when Dai acted like he'd hurt him, like he'd *ever* hurt him.

Dai wasn't a little boy any more: sitting on the bench that made up his window, he filled the whole of its frame, one knee up against his chest and the other outstretched, hanging off the end of the window seat because the bench wasn't wide enough for the full length of his leg.

His forehead was resting on the glass of the window, and he was looking down into the garden as the others played some fucking boardgame Oidhche hadn't listened to the name of when they'd invited him to play, as if he'd ever agreed to play a boardgame with them before.

Coming up to stand behind his son, he followed his gaze downward to the kids on the patio – to Ariana, who had linked arms with Trevyn, the two of them sharing a bottle of wine and laughing whenever they rolled their dice; to Gearóid and Bridie, who were both leaning forward in their seats and playing together very seriously; to Siân and Dag, who kept throwing popcorn and what looked like gummy worms at Cassian, who kept catching them and either eating them himself or dropping them into his boyfriend's mouth (Oidhche didn't know his name yet, as he had a policy of not asking the boyfriends' names until they'd been around for six months, and none of Cassian's had so far lasted more than four).

Huw was sitting aside with his own wife and Trevyn's, and from the way they kept laughing, Huw, Carlotta, and Marina altogether, they were betting each round on which team would win out.

Oidhche looked down at Dai's face.

He didn't look sad, like he wanted to go down and join them – he looked drugged out of his skull, like if he wanted to go down, he'd need one of the others to carry him.

"I'm sorry," said Dai. He slurred the word slightly, but it wasn't the stumbling stammer that Oidhche heard when his jaw was quivering – he could see Dai move his jaw after, trying to get the cotton wool numbness out of his tongue and his cheeks.

"What are you sorry for?" asked Oidhche, very quietly, and it was hard to tell if Dai heard, because his face didn't move, and he didn't even blink.

After a few seconds of this disconcerting stillness, he said, "Doesn't really matter. It's not like it'll make a difference."

Oidhche rolled his eyes.

"Do you wish it had killed me?" asked Dai, and Oidhche stared down at him.

"What, if you'd dashed your stupid little head on the cobbles?"

"No," said Dai with that chemical monotone, and now he turned his head to look up at Oidhche, his eyes dilated and his face uncomfortably blank. "The crash. If I'd died with the others."

Oidhche's hand twitched, but he didn't hit him, didn't slap the stupid little cunt across the face no matter that he wanted to: with his other hand, he gripped Dai tight by the jaw, squeezing hard enough that even through the haze from the drugs he released a sound of pain, and leaned in very close, so that their eyes were locked.

Dai didn't react like he usually would, didn't scream or cry or start to shake, but he grunted, and he fidgeted uselessly, and one of his hands, clumsy, came up to loosely pull at his father's wrist.

"You ever fucking say that to me again," whispered Oidhche, "I'll put you out of this fucking window. Do you understand?"

"But don't you? Don't you?" asked Dai, almost like he was begging for it. "Don't you wish?"

"Shut *up*," Oidhche growled, loud enough that even out of it, Dai leaned back slightly, his eyes widening. "No, you stupid little prick, I don't want you fucking dead – if I wanted you dead, I'd kill you myself. Some part of me still hopes you'll grow yourself a spine, that you'll learn to be something other than a goddamn embarrassment, but until then, I'm your father, you're my *son*, and you'll live."

"What if I don't want to?" asked Dai, and Oidhche shoved him back hard, hard enough that the back of his head made a thunk as it hit the glass.

"You try to fucking kill yourself, lad," said Oidhche, "and I'll really give you something to be fucking anxious about. I've buried enough fucking children – you can have the good graces to wait until *I* die first."

"I wish I could be better," said Dai dully, and Oidhche wondered why he'd even bothered, when it only made him fucking angry, whenever he *tried*, with Dai.

"You and me both," muttered Oidhche, and resisted the urge to slam the door as he left because he knew it made the boy jump, although he didn't know why he bothered. He closed it quietly, so that it barely made a click, and for a second, he stood there, and wondered what Saoirse would say.

Something better than what he could say – she'd always been better, with Dai, and he'd been better, he'd almost thought he could *get* better, until…

Oidhche sighed, long and slow, emptied his lungs until he felt in control, and then he went back downstairs.

* * *

A skating rink was a weird thing to adjoin a gym, Dai thought, but it had just worked out that way – in much the same way many leisure centres had their gyms overlooking the pool, this one overlooked a huge, wooden-floored arena where people would skate or rollerblade. There was another broader basement level attached, where people went with skateboards and scooters too – Siân went regularly, and had some trophies on her wall from local competitions – but Dai could see down into the skating rink from anywhere in the exercise room, because they had mirrors at a tilted angle to that people could look down into the rink the same way you could watch the TVs as you exercised.

He recognised Verdance Pike by the thick, sandy cloud of his coiled hair. When he skated on the ice, he normally wore a bobble hat to keep his hair down, but when he was skating on wheels, he tied his hair up into a thick bunny's tail that bounced as he moved.

He moved beautifully across the laminate floor, spinning now and then on his feet, and Dai sighed quietly as he watched him – Verdance Pike was frightening, but Dai liked to watch him, and Verdance had never done anything untoward to him, never threatened him. They were friends, after a fashion, and Dai genuinely liked whenever he and Verdance talked.

He was beautiful and off-putting and very strange, but there was something about Verdance that just set Dai at ease.

When Dai had been a little boy, it had been Verdance who'd taught swimming classes in the summer. Dai hadn't particularly enjoyed them, and had been slow compared to his brothers and sisters, but he'd liked the classes, and he'd liked Verdance.

Later—

He couldn't swim any more, and even as a teenager, he'd basically stopped going to classes for anything outside of the house, had been aside with a private tutor most days a week because he kept having panic attacks in the real classrooms, and he'd stopped doing anything extracurricular – he'd dropped out at fifteen, which he'd been allowed to do so long as he went to a trade school, so he'd studied culinary sciences until he'd turned seventeen.

He'd be eighteen soon.

He'd used to like roller skating, he thought – he had distant, cloudy memories of skating after his mother, holding hands with Leah and Morrigan, the three of them laughing and screaming and shouting at Tomás and Sadhbh as they ran circles around them. He could vaguely recall the sensation of the wheels under his feet, the sensation of fast motion – but most of all he could remember his sisters laughing and feeling like he belonged with his siblings, and like they wanted him to.

He got off the rowing machine, and reached up to check his eyes, but they weren't wet – his face was soaked, but it was with sweat from having been on the rowing machine for an hour, not tears.

He went to the changing room via the side of the rink for reasons he didn't want to think about, but to his relief – and maybe some uncertainty – as soon as Verdance saw him he smiled and skated over to the edge of the rink, landing against it with a thunk and hooking his hands over the railing, smiling at him.

"Hello, Dai," he said softly, tilting his head to the side in that funny, obviously inhuman way he had – everything about Verdance Pike was slightly uncanny. Like his father, he had canine teeth that slightly protruded from his mouth, their points depressing the surface of his lower lip, and he had long, point-tipped ears. His hair was thick and tightly curled, a sandy blond colour, and his skin was a warm brown, lacking the purple tint to it a lot of Pike's children had – Verdance Pike's mother was fae, and he'd been raised among fae, not humans, but somehow, he looked less fae at a glance than some of his siblings.

"Hi," he said shortly. "Back for now?"

"For a few months. My father is reshuffling some of his priorities – he has a new secretary, and is being firmly encouraged to buck up his ambitions. It brings a man joy to see, I must say."

Pike's new secretary was Gellert Osgodby.

"Any inside info you want to share?" asked Dai, and Verdance laughed.

Dai wasn't that anxious, he was distantly aware, but that was because he'd just been using machines for two hours after boxing with Cassian – Dai preferred to exercise at home, but this was the closest gym to Cassian's surgery, and Cassian had used that as an unsubtle excuse to get him out of the house for the first time in months – his whole body ached, now, and he was flooded with endorphins.

His hands were shaking, but he didn't really feel it.

"I'm afraid not, darling," Verdance said. "How about you?"

"Nah," said Dai. "Nothing I can reveal at this juncture."

Verdance smiled at him, and then he looked him up and down. "You seem remarkably well-adjusted. You're on extremely powerful medication at the moment, I take it?"

"Took a lot of tranquilizers to get me out of the house," said Dai. "Couldn't feel my mouth, barely any peripheral vision, and my reflexes were a little slow. Once I was here, I was okay. Probably going to swallow another mouthful of pills to be driven home."

"Want me to drive you?" asked Verdance.

"You have a rental car?"

"It's Rachel's, she's doing guard duty, so she doesn't need it as much."

"What's she guarding?"

"Wouldn't you like to know?" asked Verdance, and Dai felt himself laugh, and it was real, genuine. It had been a little while since he'd laughed with someone who wasn't Dag or Siân. "I assume you'd rather not shower here, even in the private booth."

Dai nodded his head.

Verdance was a weird guy – he was a Pike, and he did jobs for the Pikes, but he was friendly with a lot of people in Lashton across all kinds of family lines, and he was a personable guy, cheerful, a good judge of other people. Dai was surprised that he trusted him as much as he did, but he did.

When he'd been a teenager, Dai'd refused to do pretty much any class or session or club, no matter what Dad tried to get him to do, and whenever anyone else was doing, he'd sometimes sit aside and just... shiver in the corner, try to block out everyone looking at him.

Verdance would take him aside when he saw him, and they'd just run on the treadmills, or Verdance would time him rowing, or have Dai throw tennis balls at him so he could practice his swing on the days when Dai's grip was better.

His sister's car had red fur seats, and it made Dai laugh as he got into the passenger seat, clipping the belt over his chest. He liked it when car seats had novelty shit like that – it made him less likely to freak out over anything, for one, made the flashbacks less likely, but mostly it just looked fucking stupid, and he liked that.

"Tell me about your father's newest hunk of meat," said Verdance as he put the car in gear.

"His name's Dunnock Wesson. He's hired muscle."

"Mmm, yes, I know who he is, darling," said Verdance. "I used to teach him gymnastics – he competed all over, once upon a time. I was quite intrigued when I was informed he'd transitioned both his gender and his career. He insisted for quite the time he was a student who'd eclipse his master, but he abandoned this after I thrashed him rather soundly in a parkour event. I like to imagine I contributed to the ensuing mental breakdown."

"You're so fucked in the head," said Dai.

Verdance chuckled at that. "What a queer thing for a young man like you to say. Have you taken any tranquilizers?"

"Two."

"Your Daddy hasn't taught you it's polite to share?"

"Don't call him Daddy," said Dai, fishing out the bottle. "I don't need you fucking him as well."

"That ground is well-trodden, my dear," was the reply, and Dai let out a sound of disgust as he dropped two pills into Verdance's hand.

Verdance didn't try to touch him, kept a careful gap between their hands so they didn't even brush one another by mistake, and Dai appreciated that – he also appreciated that Verdance didn't knock them back straight away while he was driving with Dai in the car, but dropped them into the well of the dashboard for him to take later.

"Darling, you do seem quite a bit more glum than usual, and rather a lot more drugged to the gills, so please don't take offence when I ask you this," said Verdance, "but is a suicide attempt on the horizon?"

"I don't know," said Dai.

"An encouraging answer," said Verdance, tone unchanging. "Truthful, I suspect, but not comforting."

"Did you want me to comfort you?"

"Darling, you comfort with your very presence, exuding your heavily medicated haze in a sort of contagious aura," was the immediate reply, and Dai sniggered. He couldn't feel his fingers at all, but they were shaking, tremoring visibly, and whenever he moved his head, the world seemed like it was moving too slowly, tipping around him like water swirling in a bowl. "I, for one, would be dreadfully put out if you decided to kill yourself."

"Because you'd have to come all the way back home for the funeral?"

"Because I'd have to come *all this way* back home for the funeral if you did," said Verdance, as if he hadn't said anything. "What if I got word of your untimely death, and I was in Italy or something, I mean, can you imagine? I'd get such short notice, too, and have to hurry home, and find something to wear, and oh, no. It'd be very unkind of you to kill yourself when I was abroad, so don't do it then."

"Okay."

"And don't do it while I'm here in Lashton, or people will naturally assume I drove you to it."

"Got it."

"And don't do it while I'm elsewhere within the country, or people will naturally assume you did the deed whilst pining in my absence."

"So you're telling me not to kill myself at all, in case it impacts you?"

"Exactly."

"Noted. I heard you brought some mundie back with you."

"Who told you that?"

"Nobody. Bridie and Ariana were talking about it, said he'd come up with you on the train. What, you introduce him to your dad?"

Verdance laughed. "What would my father care about who I'm fucking? No, I showed him a nice time at the Crystal Market and took him to the theatre, and then I put him on the train home again. He has the Sight, you know - and I think he's quite darling. He's got no brains at all."

"How old are you?"

"I was born in 1802," said Verdance, "but about four hundred and twenty, thereabouts."

"So you're older than your own dad."

"If you put stock in things like that."

"I fucking hate faeries."

Verdance laughed, leaning his head back against the headrest. "If we wanted you to like us, darling, you would."

"What's the point in taking up with a mundie, then? Even magical humans'd die quicker than you, let alone him."

"Expose any a mundie to enough magic and they won't be a mundie for much longer," said Verdance. "If I find he suits me, I'll endeavour to keep him around. If you put any person through sufficient pressure, my dear, they will undergo dramatic change. You know that, of course."

Dai didn't laugh, but the sound that he let out was almost like one, except that it was low and bitter. He was struggling to keep his eyes closed, and he sort of sat there with them half-lidded, watching Verdance's face amidst the haze of his vision, blurred even more by his own eyelashes.

"Yeah," he said. "Guess I do. Are you scared of your dad?"

"No, but I've never had reason to be," said Verdance. "Many of my siblings are frightened of him – most people in Lashton are. You are, I'd bet."

"I've never met him."

"And yet I feel you wouldn't like to."

"No," said Dai. He'd seen pictures of Lucien Pike, and Dad talked about him often – said he was a feral animal, driven by his appetite and his cock, but that when time came to be cunning, he could be very much so, and was best avoided. The man was huge, a great bulk of a man who filled a door frame, and no matter that Dai was actually decently tall, he knew that standing beside a man like Pike, he'd look tiny.

"Were you asking because you fear my father," asked Verdance, "or because you fear yours?"

"He's my dad," said Dai lowly. "He wouldn't hurt me."

"Of course he would," said Verdance. "Hasn't he already? Hurting isn't just blows and punches, darling, you should have learned that by now."

There was a distant, hollow gnaw in the core of Dai's chest – if he could feel it properly, maybe he'd feel sick, maybe he'd sweat, maybe he'd panic about it, feel it as though it were a real, physical pain. Instead he was aware of it the same way he could be aware of something on the horizon, knowing it was there, but almost able to ignore it.

"You're nearly a man of your own now," said Verdance. "You've been on the cusp of it for quite some time, never quite tipping over the edge. If you want it, grasp it."

"Grasp what?" Dai asked impatiently, opening his eyes and looking at Verdance's face properly as they pulled up to the Laithe house. "What fucking magical thing is going to make me a man, because I know you're not saying it's me turning eighteen."

"My age of majority was fourteen," said Verdance smugly. "Or ninety-eight, depending on how you look at it."

"Jesus Christ," said Dai, and Verdance chuckled, pulling up in front of the house and unbuckling his seatbelt, turning in the seat to look across at him. Dai leaned back as Verdance reached across and opened the glove compartment, reaching in for a lolly from the pile inside. "Can I have one?"

"You won't like it," said Verdance, and Dai looked at the dark red colour of the sugar glass before glancing at Verdance's sharp, protruding teeth.

"Ugh," said Dai, and Verdance grinning at him, ripping open the wrapper and popping it into his mouth. As soon as Verdance's tongue wet it, Dai could smell it – not just the sweet, sugary smell, but the coppery one underneath it. "That's rank."

"You're really not cut out for your family's line of work, you know," said Verdance casually. "I don't say it to insult you, nor to shame you, but it's a fact of life. You lack a true taste for violence, and moreover, you lack a certain resolve."

"I have C-PTSD and a severe anxiety disorder," said Dai irritably.

"Well," said Verdance, wrinkling his nose – faeries didn't much believe in the concept of mental illness, "you're certainly mentally unsound. I don't think the company of your family is particularly conducive to repairing that unsoundness either, nor indeed rendering you more able to cope with its effects."

"And what do you think would be more *conducive* to repairing my mental unsoundness?" asked Dai. "What, go off and start using my cert in hospitality to cook breakfasts at a hotel?"

"Probably," said Verdance. "You're better at cooking breakfast, I assume, than you are at money laundering, witness intimidation, embezzling, or illegal trade." Verdance chuckled to himself. "Well, I suppose you'd be better at most things than any of those."

"They're my family," said Dai. "If I go off somewhere else, I'll be alone."

"Oh, of course," said Verdance sarcastically. "Because you're not alone at all, when you're with them. Surrounded by your relatives right this moment, in fact."

"Why do you bring it up?"

"Let me bring you out with me," said Verdance, resting his cheek on the headrest. "Hm, just for a little bit? I'm here for another month or so, but then I'm off to the Queen's Realm for some time – come along with me, why don't you? I'll find you lodgings, perhaps a bit of work, something to occupy you."

Dai narrowed his eyes at Verdance, who kept his gaze. His mother was from the Queen's Realm – she worked in the Queen's Palace as a librarian, and Dai was distantly aware that while Verdance commanded no particular influence as a result of blood or upbringing, that he was well-connected in fae realms, just like he was in human ones.

"What's the catch?" asked Dai. "Is this why you offered me a lift home?"

"Even my ulterior motives have ulterior motives, darling, you know me," said Verdance. "Aside from the fact that I'd rather you not commit yourself any further to self-destruction, because quite selfishly I rather like our time together, my mother adores mad people, and her most recent one just died."

"You want to give me to your mother as a pet?"

"I want to introduce you to my mother and see if the two of you get on," said Verdance patiently, "being as my mother only likes pets which are house-trained already, but if you *did* like my mother, you would then have someone you know in the city once I depart. There is a method to my madness, you know, which puts it rather a cut above yours."

"Thanks for that."

"The Queen is looking to branch out somewhat," said Verdance softly. "She wishes to understand human fae and humans themselves more, and someone like you would be a valuable ambassador."

Dai scowled without meaning to, his lips twisting. "Hostage?"

"No, not *hostage*," said Verdance, popping his lolly out of his mouth and giving him a very disapproving look. "If I wanted to kidnap you, I might have in a heartbeat – you came into this car with me with scarce a hesitation, I might point out. If you really don't want to come along with me to there, I can arrange for something for you virtually anywhere else, but I think you'd *like* it."

"What would I like about it?"

"The food," said Verdance. "Good, clean food – more meat, which you don't eat enough of. Strangers who'll make no judgement of you, and proper people too, not like..."

"Like me?" asked Dai, arching an eyebrow. "Humans?"

Verdance gave him a flat look, and kept talking. "And the strong magical currents are a treatment of sorts for an addled mind in themselves – everyone sleeps deeply in fae lands, you know. Even those with the most disturbed and fractured of consciousnesses rarely stir or pace the halls of their homes as you do of a night."

"Night terrors aren't *pacing the halls*, Verdance," said Dai, but he laughed as he said it.

"Everything is slower there," said Verdance softly. "Time moves like molasses, rather than as grains of sand. I wouldn't suggest it were it not that I thought it might soothe your soul."

"I don't believe in souls," said Dai.

"But you'll think about it?"

Dai took the door handle, feeling his mouth twist again, his stomach roiling with uncertainty, although it was more that he wanted maybe to accept than the offer itself, and said, "I'll think about it."

"It's all I ask," said Verdance, popping his sweet back into his mouth.

"Thanks for the lift home," said Dai, and got out of the car.

When he went into the house, Dad was leaning over Bridie as she worked on her laptop. The two of them were talking to one another about whatever was on Bridie's screen, her looking up at him to talk because she was sitting down, and when he glanced over, Dad wrapped an arm around her and squeezed her shoulder, touching his chin against the top of her head.

Dai couldn't remember a time when his father had held him like that.

"Hey, Dai," said Bridie. "You didn't shower at the gym?"

"Verdance Pike gave me a lift home," said Dai. "The Queen is up to something, he says. Is interested in learning more about humans and human fae, think that means Lashton."

"I'll look into that," said Bridie. "Thanks, Dai."

Dai nodded, and feeling a little hazier now that he was back on his feet, he began the slow climb up the stairs.

* * *

"I wish I could go after him," muttered Bridie, bouncing her knee. "But he never reacts to me like he does Dag and Siân, or Cassian. I don't even see what Cassian has that I don't – we share a *mother* in common, at least, but Cassian is—"

"Cassian hits him in the face, Bridie," said Oidhche, patting her shoulder. "He's the only one in this family who will, except the twins. Try it, and maybe he'll like you better."

"I can't box," said Bridie.

"Try it over breakfast," suggested Oidhche dryly, and Bridie laughed weakly, but she turned to look at him, crossing her arms over her chest. She opened her mouth, closed it. "What?"

"He's a fucking liability," said Bridie quietly, her mouth twisting. She didn't seem happy to say it, if anything, looked almost depressed about it. Depressed wasn't good – it implied a certain powerlessness on her part. "What the fuck do we do with him? He's not... Dad, he's not getting any better, he's getting *worse*, and he can't fucking do anything. Are we supposed to keep sending him out on more and more basic shit, seeing what he can't fuck up?"

"I don't know," said Oidhche honestly, pulling away from her and going to the fridge, pulling out the filter jug and pouring himself a glass of water. "You tell me, sweetheart. He's tried therapy, tried a different school, tries to help, tried not to help. I'm at a loss at what to suggest next, and you know I like to let you kids carve your own way."

"He's not carving," she said, closing her laptop. "He's digging, and it might not be just his own grave. We need to fucking do something about him."

Oidhche slowly turned to look at her, and he didn't put too much effort into it, just cooled his gaze and didn't blink, and when she met his gaze again, she crumpled slightly, but not as Huw would have. Bridie didn't look scared of her father, didn't look frightened of what he might do to her, if she stepped out of line: she looked sad, aggrieved. "Not like that," she said in a quiet voice. "I don't mean like that. Not with everyone... Dad, I wouldn't. I couldn't."

"Okay," said Oidhche softly, but didn't soften his eyes again until after she'd hurried out, and after she'd gone, he glanced at his phone, frowning.

When he looked out of the window, he found that there was a car with monstrously furry seat covers, inside which was sitting Verdance Pike. He looked happy and cheerful as ever, a lollipop hanging off his skilled tongue, and with his shoulders and head crammed in through the passenger window so that he could argue with him was Dunnock Wesson.

Dunnock had dropped his bag on the floor, evidently distracted on his way back into the house, and Oidhche could clearly see that he was quite angry with Pike. Pike, of course, was taking the verbal abuse with his usual cat-like satisfaction, pleased as punch to receive it and not at all bothered by its tone, content, or delivery.

Dunnock had gone rounds with Pike before, but not enough to know better: Pike's amusement was steadily making him angrier and angrier, and by the time he dragged himself out of the car to stalk inside ten minutes later, he was red in the face and glowering.

"Don't slam doors, baby," said Oidhche after Dunnock came indoors, having shut the front door so hard the walls had rattled. "It makes you look uncontrolled."

"Verdance fucking Pike," growled Dunnock, "was parked on your drive. Says he drove Dafydd home – what the fuck is he doing that for? Smug fucking prick with his fucking lolly in his mouth, what the fuck does he think he's doing, showing up here and—"

Dunnock stumbled in his speech, because Oidhche had slid a hand into his shirt, but when he realised Oidhche wasn't telling him to stop, he kept going.

"—hanging around, when he's not been fucking you in forty years and has no excuse to be here, unless he's fucking your son. Is he? Does he still think he can fuck *you*?"

Oidhche had his palm spread against Dunnock's chest, feeling the furious pound of his heart, and when Oidhche didn't say anything, just smirked at him, Dunnock scowled.

"I'm not fucking jealous," he said.

Oidhche did so like Dunnock's temper when it came out, liked the energy it brought out in him, the passion it made him fuck with. He already knew, as wound tight as Dunnock was, that he'd give Oidhche a very hard fuck later on, that he'd probably do his best to drive Oidhche directly through the mattress whilst all but wringing his neck – an appealing night of cardio was in store.

"Do you have to fucking smirk at me like that?" asked Dunnock.

"I don't have to," purred Oidhche. "But I just like you so much, baby, I just think you're so *swell*, I have to. Did you challenge him to another funny little competition, hm?"

Dunnock's lip curled.

Oidhche hadn't poked too much at those particular scabs just yet, wanted to give it time before he started touching them, playing with them. Oidhche was no expert in the exploration of one's gender – gender was something he'd thought very hard about for a summer when he was sixteen or seventeen, and then decided wasn't his business and wasn't something he wanted to concern himself with – but he was rather good, he flattered himself, at understanding and extrapolating from a timeline. Dunnock had become obsessed with Verdance Pike about a year before he'd spiralled through his meltdown, and much as Dunnock wouldn't admit to it, much as he wouldn't say so, it was plain to see from the way he held himself as a man, the way he dressed, that he was modelled in some ways on the cast of Verdance Pike, and would like to model himself further on the theme.

Oh, the differences between them were obvious, of course – Verdance Pike wasn't as tall as Dunnock was, of course, and apart from the big difference in their skin tones and facial features, Verdance half-Black fae and half-whatever Lucien Pike was even before being a fae vampire, and Dunnock white. Both of them were blond, but Pike's hair was a beautiful burst of sandy blond coils. Oidhche fondly remembered how it felt in his grip when last he'd kissed Verdance Pike, years ago when they'd almost looked the same age, but more than that, he remembered how it bounced when Pike was fucking him, all those wonderful curls tossed about whether he tied them up or not. Dunnock's hair was blond too, but it was a darker, golden colour, and when he'd first come out, he'd cropped his hair very short, almost shaved himself bald.

It was growing longer now. He liked to shave it underneath and have it long on top, like Pike kept his, and it was growing longer, little by little.

Dunnock shaved very carefully, painstakingly, although he could easily grow a moustache or even a little beard by now, but he didn't, stayed clean shaven like Pike was; Dunnock wore sports clothes and tight t-shirts and jeans, dressed himself like a mannequin in whatever was the blandest shop window, but Oidhche noticed the way he stopped sometimes and looked at certain clothes.

Ice skaters' big, billow-sleeved blouses; tight leather trousers with fancy buckles and knotted clasps; shirts and overcoats with lace under pieces. He never wore any of it, but when one of the girls or Cassian were looking through magazines that had fae models, fae fashions, he'd look. He'd pick through the pages very slowly, sometimes even trace the silhouettes under his fingers.

When Oidhche had bought him the leather jacket he always wore now, a handsome thing cropped in tight at the waist made from yellow butter cow leather, and decorated with the ephemera that fae often liked on their clothes – little symbols, embroidered patches of inscribed circles, and all that...

First looking at it, Dunnock's eyes had lit up, widening slightly, his lips parting, and his fingers had brushed the leather almost religiously, worshipfully, touching over the black shining thread that made up the metallic embroidery, the black stone buttons with their neat engravings.

It had only lasted a second before he'd scowled, looking up at Oidhche. "Where the fuck do you expect me to wear this to?" he'd demanded.

"Everybody needs a pop of colour, baby," Oidhche had replied. "It matches your hair."

He'd complained about it for a week or two, but he wore it every day, that jacket. Oidhche liked the way he looked at himself in mirrors or frosted windows when they walked past them, liked the way he'd raise his chin a little higher, and now and then he'd shift his hips like Pike did when he walked – just a few steps, just a few, just to see how he looked.

That was now, of course – as a teenager, Dunnock had just been a girl, challenging Verdance Pike to game after game that she just couldn't win, while everyone watched and thought how strange it was, that she was so obsessed.

Oidhche wondered sometimes, what Pike said to that girl who wasn't a girl and didn't know it yet – or didn't want to admit it yet – in the moments where they were alone together, or the moments where Pike could speak and other people couldn't hear what he said.

It had always been Verdance Pike's passion, to see people on the cusp of change and encourage them further along the path – Oidhche fondly remembered when he'd done the same to him.

"I'm not jealous," said Dunnock again.

"I believe you," said Oidhche sweetly, lying all the while, and pulled Dunnock closer to kiss him.

* * *

It was Huw's birthday, so they went out for a family lunch.

They did this for the whole family, most years – Trevyn and Ariana's were always done together, because their birthdays were only three days apart, but everyone else had their own date on the calendar, Dad included – Dad especially – except Dai.

They weren't birthday parties, not really. What they were was statements of family cohesion, public examples of their visibility.

Dai didn't fit in with that, when he started hyperventilating as soon as someone approached him with a lit lighter, alone a cake filled with a load of candles, when having all the attention on him freaked him out so much that he snapped. As much as he hated it sometimes, fading into the background, most of his siblings barely even looking at him throughout most dinners and lunches and meetings, it was preferable to the alternative, because as much as he wanted the attention, recognition, as soon as he got it, he couldn't cope.

He couldn't fucking cope with anything any more.

It was raining, and Dai sat in the back seat with his arms crossed over his chest, staring into space. Trevyn was asleep beside him, his head tipped back, and because of the angle his neck was at, he was snoring slightly – Marina, his wife, was working and wasn't able to come; Dag was sitting in the passenger seat, massaging his wrist, and Siân was driving.

Dag could drive, but he didn't like to during busy periods. Dag was good for night drives, or to give you a lift very early in the morning, or to take you out to the country for a solitary drive somewhere. Traffic made him nervous, made him twitch and judder, and that was even after all the therapy he'd gone to, after.

Dai couldn't remember much, had blocked most of it out – repressed it – but what he did remember was Dag stuck fast under his seatbelt, one of his arms hanging limply down. His eyes were open but his skull had been cracked, and blood had been dripping down his face, gathering at the tip of his nose before it dripped off.

Funny that he remembered Dag and thinking at the time that Dag was dying or that he was already dead, when Dag had lived – when Dai and Dag and Siân had lived, and Tomás and Morrigan and Leah and Sadhbh had died.

Dag and Siân had gone to see Gellert Osgodby, after everything, had gone to try to threaten him or something, even though Dad had told them not to, even after the family had agreed they wouldn't, and Osgodby had broken some of his fingers, and then after, Pike had taken him aside, had done... Something.

Dag had been very shaky, the past few months, after all that. He didn't have a good tolerance for pain.

"You okay?" asked Siân.

Siân had a good tolerance for pain. Siân had a good tolerance for almost everything: she was harder than Dai was, and harder than Dag, too, harder than diamond. Dai didn't know how to talk to her sometimes, because she could be inflexible, when she felt something was the right thing to do, and Dai didn't always know how to deal with that.

She cared. She just cared very— aggressively, sometimes, like now, when she asked if he was alright, and it sounded not dissimilar to when she was demanding someone pay up the money they owed.

The thought made him smile.

"Yeah," said Dai quietly. "I'm okay."

He was on just the right balance today, between the medications he'd taken and a rare good night's sleep, so much so that he felt... stable. Placid. He wasn't shaking, wasn't pivoting inside his head from one extreme to the other – he felt extremely, supremely unaffected by absolutely everything, and the result was a sensation of numbness that might have been disconcerting, if it wasn't such a relief.

It was weird, days like this, days that just felt like a perfect storm, where he saw everything clearly, where he remembered things and the memories didn't jab into his nerves like ice picks, where he could talk, and do things, and enjoy things, and not feel... crazy. Fucked in the head.

On days like this, in short, he didn't feel like himself, and there was a relief in that.

Everything would be easier, if he wasn't like himself.

"I hate it when you're like this," said Siân, and Dai's smile faded slightly, a confused frown replacing it as he caught her gaze in the rear view mirror. "All serene, like your personality's gone. Makes me miss my little brother."

"What personality?" asked Dai softly, his voice calm and even, his chest an empty pit. "What little brother?"

Siân sighed, and drove on in stony silence, Dag beside her with his face crumpled, his head turned to look out of the window. It was raining heavily outside, and the droplets of water were streaking the windows in thick rivulets as they moved.

Dai had been thinking about taking Verdance Pike up on his offer. He'd been thinking of it almost all the time, the past week, wondering if it'd be worth going along. He wasn't worried about the risk aspect, not worried about being killed or something – he wasn't that valuable, and he wasn't scared of getting killed.

He didn't like the idea of leaving Lashton, but he didn't much like being *in* Lashton either – he didn't know if he liked anything. What he knew he didn't like, though, was sitting in the same meetings and lunches every week, and knowing everybody thought he was a fuck-up who couldn't contribute – knowing he *was* a fuck-up that couldn't contribute.

Even on the rare occasions he managed to eavesdrop something good, it was hard to use it, and he wasn't made to spy or go unnoticed – people noticed someone who shook like he did, who flinched as hard as he did, who couldn't stay calm.

It was either go to the Queen's land, see what thick magic on the air did for him, or go back to therapy, and he knew how he felt about therapy, had stopped going by the time he was fourteen and refused to go back – and his dad didn't believe in therapy anyway, and hadn't made him go.

Getting in a car crash that poured glass into your rib cage while one of your brothers, three of your sisters, and the nanny who was driving all died beside you, everyone half-ripped to shreds, that fucked you up – he didn't need a therapist to understand that, and he definitely didn't need a therapist (or a counsellor, or a psychologist, or a psychiatrist) helpfully explaining that the real problem was that he didn't eat enough or that he felt bad about his body or that he was obviously a repressed faggot or that he needed to feel "validated" by his father, whatever the fuck that meant.

Dag and Siân had gone to therapy, after. He didn't know if it had actually made any difference to Siân, if it had made her feel better or not, but it had helped Dag, he thought.

He didn't actually know.

He didn't tend to ask.

Too much of the shit around therapy seemed to be about making you feel "better in yourself", and he didn't know what the fuck that meant, because he'd never felt "good in himself" but he didn't think he'd felt *bad* in himself" either – and it was hard. And it hurt.

And everything was hard enough and hurt enough already.

"Wake up, Trev," said Dai, nudging Trevyn in the side, and Trevyn blinked sleepily awake, sitting up in his seat.

Dai got out of the car as soon as they pulled up, not waiting for Trev to wake up enough to follow them in, and he jogged under the canopy in front of the restaurant's front door, stepping inside.

The long table was already set up, and Cassian and his boyfriend were already sitting down, as were Bridie, Ariana, and Gearóid. Huw and Carlotta hadn't arrived yet, and nor had Dad.

Dai didn't even scan the restaurant, didn't even look around *for* people particularly – it was just that Osgodby was sat in direct view of the door, and caught his gaze even though he wasn't looking particularly. Looking at him, something inside Dai shifted from placid neutrality to sudden, scorching fury.

He was sitting back in the booth, one of his legs crossed over the other, and he was picking at whatever was on his plate: before Dai could stop to think about it, before he could even consider what he was doing, he was marching forward.

He didn't even know what he wanted to do, wanted to say – he just wanted to say *something*, just wanted to say something to the man who'd fucking humiliated him and never been punished for it at all, never experienced any kind of recompense because he'd picked someone big to hide behind, and he was in the right head space, was ready to say it, was *ready*—

Gellert Osgodby wasn't sitting alone.

There was a bunch of massive blokes around the table with him, Pikes – and right next to him, huge as anything, sitting back in a big chair, was Lucien Pike himself.

Dai froze like a deer in headlights, rooted to the spot, and he couldn't even get himself to turn around, couldn't get himself to move, to say anything, to speak – he needed to go, needed to fucking turn the fuck around, needed...

"Hello, Mr Laithe," said Osgodby calmly, standing to his feet as if to greet him, as if they were friends, and as much as part of him raged at it, a significant part of Dai lurched with a sort of desperate relief. "My apologies, Mr Pike, I'll—"

"This the Laithes' youngest?" asked Pike. He had an East End accent, sounded like a Londoner even though he was however many centuries old and had been in Lashton most of that time – in Pike's face, which was hard-chiselled and strong, Dai saw some of the features he knew from Verdance Pike's, knew from other Pikes around town. Pike's protuberant canine teeth were long and sharp, and his eyes were deep and round and focused purely on Dai. "Dafydd?"

"Sorry," Dai managed to get out, leaning back to stumble away. He felt like he'd been plunged in ice water, his chest breaking out into a painful ache even though his hands still didn't shake, even though his teeth weren't chattering. He felt terror in a distant, indescribable way: mostly, he just felt shooting pain through the whole of his body, and in his head, all he could hear was wrenching metal and thick, dripping liquid. "Thought I saw someone I knew," he said hurriedly, his voice echoing in his own ears, not sounding like it was coming out of his own mouth, sounding too far away for that. "I'll just—"

"*Ah!*" said Pike.

The next moment condensed to three flashes of understanding. Dai distantly understood that Pike was talking, but his voice just turned to blurry noise as it came into Dai's ears: what he did know, what he did feel, was one of Pike's strong fingers catching his belt loop, the sharp tug as Pike pulled him closer, and how cold and hard and frighteningly big Pike was underneath him, when Pike pulled him into his lap.

Dai was shaking now.

He was so aware of the blood in his face that he felt like he was about to start bleeding from his eyes, and his throat felt ragged from wanting to suddenly throw up. Even through the haze of the tranquilisers, he felt such huge, overwhelming terror that something just...

Broke in him.

He couldn't talk. He couldn't really hear what Pike was saying, or Osgodby – he was aware that Pike was touching him, aware that he was reacting, that he was making horrible, embarrassing noises, aware that Pike's friends were laughing at him.

It felt like it went on for hours, Pike's hands sliding over his thighs, under his shirt, and he wanted to scream, wanted to beg for help, but he couldn't concentrate, couldn't even move. He wasn't in control of his body, not any more, was just riding in it, and he wondered if Pike was going to actually rape him, if this was how he'd lose his virginity, just in a restaurant, just with Pike touching him, and not even be able to say anything.

He couldn't breathe.

He was breathing, maybe, but also, he couldn't, and everything hurt, and everything was shattering and there was blood pouring down his chin from where he'd bitten his lips, and he wasn't in Pike's lap any more when Dad, in front of him, said, "Jesus *Christ*."

"Daddy," Dai whispered, his voice coming out in a ragged sob.

Dag and Siân were holding him up to keep him from falling, and Dai didn't know where they were, because it was dark, and everything was blurry except his father's face.

Dad reached out, pressing his handkerchief against the blood dribbling down Dai's chin, and then Dai was off the floor, because his father had picked him up the ground, and Dai passed out completely.

* * *

Oidhche leaned on the balcony, his vape pen in one hand and a glass of mead in his other hand. It was strong stuff, spiced with cinnamon – he didn't get it out too often, but of all the nights, now was one of them.

Behind him, he heard his phone ring again, and he turned to glance back at it. It was Huw's ringtone, and Dunnock didn't even turn to look at it properly. He turned over from where he'd fallen asleep on the sofa, yawning, and declined the call without even looking at the screen, dropping his head onto the cushions again.

The rain had dropped off for now, but it was going to rain again soon, he thought, and he didn't even care. If it rained on him, so be it: the linen of his suit would turn transparent, but now that cigarettes were all but outlawed, he didn't have to worry about what he was smoking – vaping – going out.

Dai had looked bad, earlier.

Glassy-eyed, shaking, soaked with sweat, blood pouring out of his mouth and dripping down his chest, Dai hadn't even been able to keep himself standing, had hung loosely between the twins with his feet not solid underneath him, and for a terrifying second, Oidhche had thought he was already dead.

He'd carried him back out to the car that hadn't yet pulled away again, and Dunnock, who'd been talking with the driver, turned back to look at him, glanced down to Oidhche's son fainted in his arms, and said, "Drive. Back to the house."

When Dai had come to, he hadn't spoken. He was completely shut down, buried somewhere deep within his own head, his eyes open and staring, and Oidhche had wrapped him tightly in a blanket once he'd gotten him inside as Dunnock had pulled off his shoes, and for a while, he'd sat with the boy between his knees, Dai's head against his chest.

Dai had been uncomfortably cold for such a big lad, and a part of Oidhche had distantly wondered what Saoirse would call it – shock? Disassociation? Trauma response? - with her big fancy medical words, but the time for wondering what his wife would say to x or y was over. He wrapped Dai tighter in the duvet, pulled Dai in close, and for the first time in the longest time, he held Dai against his chest, even though he *was* shaking.

It wasn't at Oidhche, of course – Dai was so buried in his own fucking head, in whatever Christ-fucked fugue Pike had sent him into, that he was likely barely even cognizant of Oidhche at all, and Oidhche just held the boy and ached.

He'd wondered, holding him like that, shaking like a leaf as Dunnock made up a hot water bottle for him, a kettle of cocoa for Dai to drink later – Dunnock regularly went to the first aid classes Cassian taught on his free evenings, but something told Oidhche that he knew this for himself more than for random victims.

Cradling his youngest boy's head in his hands, his nose pressed into Dai's hair, he'd wondered if it wouldn't be kinder to snap his neck now, and be done with it. He'd hated the idea as soon as it had come into his head, because it had made dampness prick at the corner of his eyes, and whilst Oidhche wasn't a man who was ashamed of tears – he liked to be fucked too hard to shy away from wet eyes – he didn't like the sign of how hard it was hitting him.

Maybe it would be kinder, but that didn't matter: he couldn't kill one of his own babies, not after losing four of them already, not even when it would be a kindness, not even when he was suffering, not even when he knew he was impacting the family as a whole.

There was Oidhche's weakness, at the core of things.

Dai had come awake enough, after an hour or two, to start crying. It had been a pitiful sound, ragged and rough and *loud*, and Oidhche had wrapped him more tightly in the blanket, wrapped his arms around his chest and held him as tightly as he dared, until the sobbing stopped, and Dai wasn't passed out, but asleep.

He was in Oidhche's bed now, asleep with his face pressed into Oidhche's silk pillows instead of his own, but Oidhche itched at the thought of putting him back in his own room, putting him out of where Oidhche could see him, watch him, make sure no one else was touching him – making sure he wasn't alone and crying over it, or hurting himself.

The phone rang again, and Oidhche stalked back into the other room to pick it up.

"What?" he demanded, and he heard Huw flinch on the other end of the line.

"Dad," he said softly, *almost* reproachfully, but not quite. "Are you coming to join us?"

"You're thirty-nine, sweetheart," said Oidhche softly. "I think you'll survive one birthday without me there."

There was silence on the other end of the line, and then Huw asked, in a quiet voice that was entirely without rancour, "Is he okay?"

"No," said Oidhche.

"You want us to come home?"

"What, get everyone to cuddle on the bed together, like we did when his mother was alive?" asked Oidhche softly. "All of you kids in a big pile, him in the middle, the baby, like he used to be? Back when he could stand any of us looking at him for a second, when he could bear one of us touching him? Back when something as simple as watching a movie didn't send the kid spiralling?"

Huw could have responded to that by telling Oidhche he was being weak and sentimental – he could do, easily. If Huw had said something like that to Oidhche, it was what *he'd* say. Huw didn't say anything.

"Enjoy your birthday, baby," said Oidhche. "I'm sorry I'm missing it – we'll go to the barber's and lunch together next week, huh? Just us boys."

"I'm nearly forty, Dad, I'm not a boy any more – and nor are you."

"That mean you're too good to get your hair cut with your daddy?"

"Nah," said Huw. "You want us to rough Pike up?"

"Don't try it, sweetheart. That's not a scuffle you can win."

"You could," said Huw, and Oidhche laughed softly, turned to Dai in the bed.

"Your daddy's only human, Huw, and he's getting old just like you are," said Oidhche softly. "Can't let yourself forget that." He tossed the phone aside before he got onto the bed, lying on the other side of the pillow from Dai, leaving a gap between them. He wanted to reach out, to close the gap, to hold him to his chest, but Dai was fast asleep, and he didn't want to interrupt that.

The night terrors woke all of them up, anyway, less than an hour later.

* * *

It was a Monday, and the meeting was family only, except for Cerys, his dad's secretary, and Dunnock.

Dunnock was sharpening knives at his dad's left side, and Dai was sitting back in his seat. He was wrapped in his coat still, because he was cold as Hell even though the day was mild, and he wasn't looking at anybody to save him from the way everyone kept quietly suggesting that *after last night*, maybe he should go home and take it easy. Maybe, everyone kept saying, he should just relax, do something fun, not come to a meeting.

The night terrors last night had been the worst he'd had in a long time.

He didn't really remember anything from the restaurant, and what he did remember was fractured and came to him in a strange, out of order slide show – Pike touching him, seeing Osgodby from across the room, his dad's face, Dag picking him up, a car ride, someone – probably Dag, maybe Siân – wrapping him in a duvet.

Crying.

He remembered crying a lot.

He'd screamed so loud last night that he'd hurt his voice, and he'd woken up on the landing when Dunnock had grabbed him, drenched in sweat and piss and tears, just before he'd gone over the bannister and hit the bottom landing.

It wasn't the worst drop, only twelve feet, and the first time he'd done it his mother had had that patch of floor carpeted and enchanted to soften the hit, but it was still dangerous, depending on what position you fell in.

He'd woken up with a sharp gasp, and Dunnock had pulled him back from where he'd almost fallen over the railing by a grip around the waist, letting him go so that he could scramble into the bathroom to peel off his clothes and get washed off.

He hadn't even tried to go back to sleep after, just started prepping for breakfast.

The meeting went on around him, and he didn't really listen, didn't even try. He hadn't been at Huw's birthday lunch, but he could be here, and not do anything fucking crazy for once, but he could *be* here, and then...

And then maybe he'd text Verdance Pike.

He kept watching Dunnock as he slid his whetstone over his set of knives. Dunnock, with his perfect blond hair and his perfect chiselled jaw and his perfect body, his beautiful hands and beautiful, haughty attitude, Dunnock, who a therapist would probably say Dai was just repressed about wanting to fuck, and who gave a shit who he wanted to fuck anyway? When was Dai, realistically, ever going to be together enough to fuck anybody, unless Pike or some other big bloke decided they'd fuck *him*, in which case, he'd get no choice in the matter, so why even think about it?

He didn't know if that would actually happen.

His hands weren't shaking, and he wasn't really in a place to judge whether that was good or not, because he also couldn't really control what his eyes focused on, and he couldn't hear anything in the room over the sound of grinding metal in his head – the sound, he was distantly aware, of a fire-fighter's spreader-cutter moving through metal.

He hated that fucking sound, but hating it never seemed to make it go away.

Dai watched Dunnock work.

He was good with knives, worked with a variety of them – Dai had seen him fight, once or twice, seen the way he moved. Even when he was fighting, he fought like a gymnast. It was beautiful and dangerous and terrifying, and he dodged it easily whenever anyone else tried to land a blow, could gut people easily.

Dai knew how to look after knives, and he knew knife work.

On the days when there were no tremors, he was really good with his hands, and he was really good with knives, could dice things extremely quickly, do complicated little table carvings, and he didn't care much about doing pumpkins, but every Halloween, at least one of his brothers or sisters would ask him to do a design for them that they couldn't execute themselves.

He wondered what it would feel like, actually stabbing someone, actually killing someone, if he could just get over the fucking spinelessness – would he be able to, if he went to the Queen's City, and spent a few months, a few years, a few centuries maybe, there? Would he be better?

He'd never be normal.

But would he be better? Would he *feel* better?

It was hard to imagine, but tempting.

"And I'm worried about the Renns and the Sorrels," said Dad, loudly enough that it somehow cut through the haze in Dai's ears, and Dai turned to look at him. Everyone was looking at him, and around the table it was all serious faces, focused expressions.

"What are you worried about?" asked Bridie. "Dad, I know they're part of the main five, but we all know that they're not in the main three. It really comes down to us, the Pikes, and the Kings – the Renns and Sorrels—"

"And what if they stop being the Renns and Sorrels?" prompted Dad. "Their kids hang out together, don't they, hm? Dag, Siân, Dai, the kids they went to school with, they mix together. Where's the separation?"

"Only because they go to the same schools," said Huw, leaning forward. "Dad, you know yourself, all of us were friends at school — how many times did I bring Lance Pike home after we'd been playing rugby together? Hell, Courageous King was one of Cassian's first boyfriends."

"In groups?" asked Dad. "Outside of sports teams or events you were going to, would two or three of any of you ever meet up with two or three members of the Pikes or the Kings, hm?"

Dai looked around the table, at the way all of them were silent, thoughtful. The Renns and Sorrels were banding more together, if Dad thought about it like that — part of the reason Dai had been so desperate to drop out of school was because he'd get six of them, mixed

Renns and Sorrels, coming after him at once. They'd never touch him — they knew what would happen to them, if they tried to touch him, knew that one of his brothers or sisters would rip them apart — but they'd... *talk*, and that was worse.

"That generation," said Dad softly, "is going to be dangerous if they intermarry. If the Renns and the Sorrels become one family, if they unite their holdings, that's dangerous. With Pike's new business approach, the expansion, the new sense of strategy, the Kings are anxious to prove their superiority, and while that anxiety leaves gaps in their defences and in the market, what we don't want is for the Kings and Pikes to push the Renns and Sorrels closer together."

"So we start messing around on their turfs, try to pin it on the other family?" asked Huw, but around the table, Dai saw others shaking their heads.

"It could backfire if we try to run interference between them," said Dag. "I know that's the traditional thing, to get two families fighting by making miscommunications, but like, we're too connected, social media-wise — it's too easy to verify, to see through it."

"You think?" asked Dad.

"Yeah, Dad," said Dag. "I think it's part of why they can be closer — they have group chats, they're in closer contact. Even though there's the physical distance between territory and stuff, the contact is instantaneous, and they record everything on their phones."

Dai thought about Miri Sorrel and Gus Renn recording him fallen on the ground outside of the wholesaler's — there were maybe twelve Sorrels that were from his generation, and six Renns, but Dad was right. They really did hang together in big groups, and he was pretty sure they all met up for parties on the regular — all of them were under twenty-five, and there was like an eight year-gap between them and the next Sorrels in age, and fifteen between them and the next youngest Renns.

They all hung out together in groups, though, which was the main thing — if they just killed a big group of them at once, so that the both of them blamed the other family for what appeared to be an accident, or even what appeared to be a fight?

Even —

"It might be advantageous to kill a large group of them," said Dunnock thoughtfully, and Dai turned to look at him. His whetstone had gone still on one of the knives, and he looked around the table. "What better to sow the seeds of discord than some sort of poison?"

"You want to spike their punch at a party?" asked Cassian.

"Not with something that'll directly kill them," said Dunnock. "We could actually kill two birds with one stone if we combine some of Pike's new fairy dust into the matter — my idea is that we take a group of them and hit them with a gas or some other poison that prompts a rage or a violence. Have Renns rip to shred Sorrels, and vice versa — grief is a powerful catalyst when it comes to stoking feelings of enmity, but not more so than apparent enmity in the first place."

Dai's mouth opened slightly, staring at Dunnock.

The anger he felt was distant until Dad said, voice warm and sweet as honey, "Oh, sweetheart, you're just doing a good job from every angle today. That's *inspired*." Dai watched the way his dad's fingers slid over Dunnock's jaw, gently chucking under his chin.

Dunnock laughed his weird, hoarse chuckle, going back to sharpening his knife, and Dai watched without really hearing it as everyone's mouths moved — Cassian was talking, spreading his hands and gesticulating, and then Huw, and then Bridie, and then Huw, and then Bridie, and they were arguing.

Dai watched Dunnock, watched his self-satisfied smile as he kept sharpening his blade. Everyone else was distracted — it was only Dunnock who noticed when Dai reached across and picked one of the blades Dunnock had already sharpened out of his leather case, and Dunnock turned slightly in his seat to look at Dai, raising one eyebrow.

"You like the weight of it?" he asked in an undertone. He'd been weirdly nice to Dai this morning, when he'd stayed for breakfast, kept saying thank you — it had been creepy, off-putting. It was because he'd seen whatever state Dai was in last night, and it was worse than him being superior. "That one isn't envenomed, but the quillions are—"

He looked so surprised, choking, and the blade was extremely sharp, and Dunnock's grip was good today: Dunnock's throat tore open easily under the knife, and with his trachea perforated, the blood bubbled as it poured out of his throat. Dai moved the knife until he hit bone, and then he thrust more weight into it — he didn't sever the vertebrae, knew cutting someone's spine was harder than that, but he knew he'd hit nerves when Dunnock's whole body spasmed, and the whetstone and the other blade clattered to the floor.

They were shouting now.

Everyone was shouting, and there were hands around Dai's shoulders, hauling him back from Dunnock, Siân and Dag shouting in his ears, and Dai laughed, because the blood that poured over his hands was warm and thick and not sticky just yet, and he could see the light going out of Dunnock's eyes as they went blank and dark, and he slid out of his chair with his throat so wrenched open that Dai could see the white pieces of spine.

Dai felt... Powerful.

Satisfied, yes, satisfied and triumphant and fiercely happy, but most of all, he felt *powerful*. His blood was surging under his skin, making his skin feel on fire, and as he watched Cassian try to heal Dunnock, he knew he wouldn't be able to — here he was, killing a man and beating Cassian outside of the ring on the same day.

"What?" he asked, laughing, as Dag wrenched the knife out of his hand. "You kept telling me to relax, have some fun today!"

* * *

It was the sudden movement that made Oidhche turn his gaze over, and it happened so quickly that even if he'd wanted to do anything, he probably couldn't: Dai was quick with a knife, and he carved out Dunnock's throat like he was carving a turkey, quick movements of the blade that sent flesh dropping down to his chest in a heavy drop of thick, nasty wetness, and Oidhche could see just in that — what, two seconds? Three? — that Dunnock was already dead, that there was nothing Cassian would be able to do.

It was a shame, but it was what it was: these things happened.

What Oidhche cared about was not the look on Dunnock's face, a face which was rapidly paling from the blood loss, at his wide eyes, his spasming body; he didn't much care about the chaos, about all of the kids shouting and getting to their feet, at the twins hauling their brother back from his first victim and taking the knife off him, or Cassian throwing himself over the table to wrap his hands around Dunnock's open throat to try to stem the bleeding.

What he cared about was Dai, spattered with arterial spray and with a hand and arm so soaked with thick blood it looked as though he'd dipped it in a vat of the stuff, Dai's hand completely steady, Dai laughing, Dai *grinning*.

A real, wide grin.

No fear, no anxiety, no tremoring — just a pure, perfect grin.

He hadn't seen Dai grin like that since he was a little boy, and Dai had just *killed* someone.

Finally, for the first time, the kid had gotten his hands dirty, killed a man — and judging by that laugh, judging by the way he was taunting his big brother, judging by his toothy smile, he *liked* it.

There was a potential in that.

"Well, look at that," said Oidhche, and over all the chaos, none of the kids seemed to be listening to him — none of them except Dai, who looked straight at him as the twins hauled him backward, out of the room. "Guess you're your daddy's son after all."

Dai stared at him, and then his grin widened. "You don't want me to say fucking sorry?" he demanded — didn't even stutter, didn't even look away.

"Baby, you say sorry, I'll have you prosecuted for that," said Oidhche, and he ignored the way Bridie hissed, "Dad!" at him, the way Dag looked at him with disgust: what mattered was the way it made Dai laugh harder, even as he went along with Dag and Siân, letting them pull him out of the room to drip blood into the hallway.

"The fuck is wrong with you?" demanded Bridie. "He just fucking *killed* someone!"

"Exactly, sweetheart," said Oidhche, getting to his feet and reaching over, carefully taking the leather jacket he'd given Dunnock off the back of the boy's chair. It was a little bloody, but that would wash off, and Dai would like a trophy — the same couldn't be said, unfortunately, for Oidhche's linen shirt, in which he expected the droplets of blood would stay forever.

As he'd suspected, Dunnock was not proving possible to revive, although Cassian was of course still trying.

"Exactly?" repeated Bridie.

"Means he's finally one of us," said Oidhche. "Caught up with the rest of the family."

"He's fucking gone crazy," said Bridie.

"He was already crazy, Bride," said Oidhche. "But that, that's... mmm, that's *potential*."

"I thought you liked Dunnock," said Bridie softly.

"Of course I did," said Oidhche. "But I didn't love him — I love you." He cupped her cheek, and watched her expression change, watched her think about it for a second, glancing over the chaos and out of the windows. Dai was nowhere in sight — the twins had taken him somewhere to hose him off. "My babies always come first, Bridie. You know that."

"He could be more of a liability like this," said Bridie.

"Maybe," said Oidhche: he couldn't stop smiling. "But if he can do that to someone outside of this room? The liability'll be *worth* it."

Bridie narrowed her eyes, but she was a visionary, and he could see that: her lips shifted into something that wasn't quite a smile, and he kissed her on the top of her head before he passed her by.

* * *

Forty minutes later, when Dai was towelling off his hair, calmer and not laughing uncontrollably any more, he went into his dad's office.

"You should take his jacket," said Dad, and Dai looked at the yellow leather jacket laid over the cushion of the chaise where Dunnock often sprawled. It was clean of blood, and Dai looked between it and his father, cautious. "Oh, don't be like that, baby — it's not like it'll fit anybody else."

"Thanks," said Dai.

His father moved forward, and Dai didn't know what to make of the smile on his face, didn't know if he should flinch back or away.

Murder, it turned out, was a pretty big high, but it had set off the equilibrium he'd managed to settle at — his hands were shaking again, and Dad picked up his hands, squeezing them. Dai swallowed, glancing down at the floor.

"What, you thought a little murder would cure you?" asked his father. "I'm sorry, sweetheart, but there's a reason none of your therapists suggested that."

"It felt good," said Dai.

"It does," said Dad. "Feels powerful, huh?"

Dai nodded, and when his father's hands came up to touch his cheeks instead of his hands, he did flinch, but not hard. He met his father's gaze as his eyes searched Dai's face, and he knew already, from old pictures, how much they looked alike, but he wondered if that was how his father felt, looking at him like this.

His dad pulled his head forward, and Dai wasn't sure what to make of it until his father's lips brushed the top of his head.

Dai smiled against his father's chest.

"I don't know if I can do it again," he admitted in a quiet voice. It was honest, and he wondered if his father would shove him away, but he didn't. He squeezed Dai's shoulders, and as he leaned away, he patted Dai's back.

"Do you want to?" asked Dad softly, and Dai nodded his head. "Then we'll get you there, baby."

"Verdance Pike invited me to go with him to the Queen's City," said Dai. "To live there."

Dad's expression was unreadable as he studied Dai's face. "You going to?" he asked slowly.

"No," said Dai. "Not anymore."

His dad, after a few moments' pause, chuckled softly. "That's my boy," he said softly, cupping Dai's cheek, and pulled away, heading back to his desk. "Let's talk business. You know where we're at with the real estate portfolio at the moment?"

Dai stared at his father's retreating back, and although his hands were shaking distantly, his chest aching a little, that stuff almost faded into the background. He didn't think his father had ever talked to him about this stuff before.

"Uh, in Camelot, Llallwg, or here in Lashton?" he asked.

His father smiled, not *at* Dai, but almost to himself, and then looked up at the old family photo on the wall, the one where they were all together — that was a year before the crash, before everything. In the photo, Dai was in his mother's arms.

"Let's talk about everything," said his father, gesturing for him to sit, and Dai did, stroking his fingers over the leather of Dunnock's jacket — his jacket, now.

Outside, it was a clear day — later on, it would become a dark, starless night.

Dai and his father talked until it was.
FIN.

More from the Author

If you'd like to seek out more of my work, *Heart of Stone* is a full-length novel set in the 18th century, and is a slowburn slice-of-life romance between a vampire and his secretary, the vampire ADHD and the secretary autistic. It has a lot of humour and domestic elements throughout.

My most recent release, *Powder and Feathers*, is a long-form contemporary dark romance with a great many fantasy elements, featuring a fucked-up dynamic between a Fallen angel and a depressed artist he begins stalking in the park.

If you're interested in perusing more novella-length pieces and short stories, I publish a huge variety of short stories that are available on a subscription model from Patreon[1] or as part of your Medium[2] subscription!

I normally publish at least one new piece a week, whether that's short stories, longer form short stories like this one, serial updates for my chaptered works, or non-fiction pieces like essays and analyses.

My name is Johannes T. Evans on both sites.

My website: www.JohannesTEvans.com[3]

My Twitter: @JohannesTEvans[4]

And finally, if you'd like to get regular email updates from me, with media recommendations, links to my most recently published work, and other little announcements, you can sign up at www.buttondown.email/JohannesTEvans.

---

1. https://www.patreon.com/JohannesEvans

2. https://johannestevans.medium.com/directory-of-work-6291c6e102b9

3. http://www.JohannesTEvans.com

4. https://twitter.com/johannestevans

www.ingramcontent.com/pod-product-compliance
Lightning Source LLC
Chambersburg PA
CBHW051301160726
47994CB00003B/1265